R & B R

5-16

9

GAMBLER'S INSTINCT

Other books by S. J. Stewart:

Vengeance Canyon
Shadow of the Gallows
Outlaw's Quarry
Beyond the Verde River
Blood Debt
Fire and Brimstone

GAMBLER'S
INSTINCT

•

S. J. Stewart

AVALON BOOKS
NEW YORK

Published by Thomas Bouregy & Co., Inc.
160 Madison Avenue, New York, NY 10016

Library of Congress Cataloging-in-Publication Data

Stewart, S. J.
   Gambler's instinct / S. J. Stewart.
      p. cm.
   ISBN 978-0-8034-9901-0 (acid-free paper)
   I. Title.

PS3569.T473G36 2008
813'.54—dc22   2007047388

PRINTED IN THE UNITED STATES OF AMERICA
ON ACID-FREE PAPER
BY HADDON CRAFTSMEN, BLOOMSBURG, PENNSYLVANIA

Dedicated to the memory of my foster father,
L. Lee Baker

Chapter One

Jake Lockridge paused on a rise that overlooked the dusty town of Piedmont. To his way of thinking, no one was apt to brag about the place. A double row of businesses bellied up against a dirt road, while a few clusters of houses squatted on side streets. But he had a hunch that he'd finally catch up with Miguel, his wandering brother-in-law, and his hunches were usually right. From what he'd learned at the last town, he knew he was getting close. Trail-weary, he felt older than his twenty-five years. He wanted nothing more than to be home with his wife and baby daughter. But Alicia was worried about her brother. It was some kind of woman's instinct, he supposed. And so she'd sent Jake to find and fetch Miguel home.

While the horses took a breather, he wiped a layer of windblown grit from his stubble-covered face. Even though it was well into September, it was still plenty

1

hot in Arizona Territory. At least in the daytime. His wide-brimmed hat protected his angular features from the ravages of the sun, but he had a thirst that called for a tall drink.

"Come on, boy," he urged the dun. "There's a bait of oats waiting for you down there."

A quarter of an hour later he was entering the town. In many places a siesta was taken during the heat of the afternoon. Not so in Piedmont. Not that anyone would have been able to sleep. The pounding of hammers jarred the peace of the community. It was plain to see what urgent need required such unnatural industry. Three men labored to build a scaffolding. It was obviously to be a gallows. Jake noted that they'd placed it directly in front of the jail so the guest of honor wouldn't have far to walk. A couple of loudmouthed spectators had nothing better to do than to watch the progress and throw out suggestions. Jake found the whole thing distasteful. No one knew better than he that there were men so murderous they needed to die. He accepted that. But such an event shouldn't be turned into a circus.

He reined up in front of the nearest saloon and swung down from the saddle. There, he tied the dun and the blood bay to the hitch rail and stretched the soreness from his lanky frame. For about the hundredth time that day, he wished he was back at his ranch with Alicia and baby Lucinda. Wishing did not a particle of good. No doubt about it, in-laws could be a pain in the backside.

The interior of the Palo Verde Saloon had seen a lot

of wear. Still, he'd been in worse. Most noticeable was the bullet hole in the mirror behind the bar that had caused a spiderweb of cracks to splinter from the center. Another bullet had plowed a furrow across the bar counter. Both scars were old.

"What'll you have?" asked the aproned barkeep.

"Got any food? It's been a while since I've had the pleasure."

"If you're not particular, I've got beans and corn bread."

"Fine. I'll take 'em."

The barkeep hollered the order, then turned his attention back to Jake.

"I expect you rode in to see the hangin' that's to take place tomorrow," he said. "Like them fellers over there." He nodded toward half a dozen men who filled one corner of the room. They looked to be passing the time with cards and whiskey before the real entertainment started.

"Nope," said Jake. "Didn't get an invite."

"Might as well stay on then. A kid shot one of the Thurstons. Wade to be exact." Then in a low voice he confided, "If you ask me, Wade wasn't much account. But he was old man Thurston's pick of the litter."

The name sounded vaguely familiar.

"Any witnesses?"

"Sure. Leastwise, he told it in court that he was. It was the dead man's brother, Ben."

Suddenly it came to Jake what he'd heard about the Thurston outfit.

"Why, even down toward Phoenix, where I'm from,

there's talk of the Thurstons. It's said they have a bad habit of walking all over folks. They always seem to get their own way."

The barkeep glanced nervously around the room.

"A word to the wise," he said in a voice that was barely audible. "Watch what you say around Piedmont. Your mouth can get you beat up—or worse."

A toothless old woman came hobbling in from a back room with his meal. He paid for it, adding an additional coin. She scooped it up and left.

"Don't worry," Jake told the bartender, "I don't plan on sticking around here any longer than I have to."

"Might be wise. Old Matt Thurston will be keeping an eye on strangers until he gets that kid hung good and proper. Says he's going to feed his carcass to the coyotes."

"Nice fellow," said Jake between bites. He found himself sympathizing with the kid. "By the way, how'd it come for this kid to shoot Wade Thurston, anyway?"

"It was robbery, pure and simple. Leastwise, that's the way Ben tells it. He stole the money Wade got for selling off some cattle. Nigh onto three hundred dollars, it was told."

"Then I guess they recovered the money, seeing as how the prisoner never got a chance to spend any of it."

Again, the barkeep glanced at the others and lowered his voice. "Nope. Strange as it sounds, they never did. The kid didn't have it on him. They claim that he hid it somewhere before he was caught. Sheriff Gillaspy tried awful hard to beat it out of him, but couldn't. Guess the boy will take the secret to the grave, that is, if he's guilty. That trial of his was a farce, with the judge drunk as a skunk. The way I look at it, the only reason it was held was to give a lynching the appearance of being legal."

Jake didn't like what he was hearing. "Maybe we should go and have a talk with the sheriff and the judge," he said. "Tell them what we think about this lynching."

"Afraid what we think don't count, Mister. It's too bad, too, 'cause the prisoner is a good-looking Mex kid. He can't be more'n seventeen."

Jake froze, his fork halfway to his mouth.

"What's his name?" he asked, dreading the answer.

"Heard it was Miguel Sandoval. Claims he didn't steal that money or kill Thurston, either one. Claims he's already got more money than he knows what to do with."

Jake tried to keep his hand steady as he put the fork down. So this was where his search for Miguel was ending.

The barkeep noticed his reaction. "Friend, you look like you just seen a ghost."

Jake met his questioning gaze. "I've changed my mind about leaving Piedmont. I think I'll stick around for a while."

"Then I'd advise you to keep out of Matt Thurston's way."

"Thanks for the warning."

He finished eating and left the saloon.

At the Piedmont Hotel, he asked a bespectacled desk clerk for a room. The man looked up at Jake who was a good six inches taller.

"I'm afraid the rooms are all reserved, sir. I'm truly sorry. Mr. Thurston and his group are coming in for the hanging that's to take place tomorrow. You might try the livery stable."

"I see," he said. "I'll do that."

Outside the hotel, he glanced at the rising gallows that was to take Miguel's life come morning. So Matt Thurston was having everything his own way. *Well, there's one thing he isn't going to have—Miguel's neck in his confounded noose.*

He led the horses down to the livery stable and made arrangements for their care, as well as a place for himself to spend the night.

"Guess you're here for the hanging," said the young hostler.

"Isn't everyone?" he replied, his voice thick with sarcasm.

"Well, it sure seems like it. I've been kept busy all day. Frankly, I'll be glad when it's over and done with."

Jake let the subject drop. He went to the front doorway of the stable where he could see the entire street. Down in front of the jail, a short, burly man lounged against the adobe wall while he watched the workmen. Light glinted off the badge on the front of his shirt.

Jake thought of Alicia back home, and how worried she was about her brother. He was thankful that she couldn't know what was happening.

While he stood there, his hat pulled low, six horsemen rode into town. The bulk and arrogance of the lead rider left no doubt that he was Matt Thurston, head bull of the herd. Three others looked enough like him to be his sons. With them was an older man. He had an air of authority too. Trailing along at the rear was a young fellow of slight build, hardly more than a kid. He didn't look at all like the Thurstons. In their wake, a dust devil whirled its way across the street, stirring up dirt and debris. It was like an evil omen.

As the Thurston outfit paraded down the street, they seemed to enjoy the stir they were causing. Except for the fellow at the tail end who looked like he'd lost his best friend. When they got to the jail, they reined up.

"You there," Thurston said, pointing to one of the carpenters. "Hurry up with that platform. Do I have to climb down from this horse and build the gallows myself?"

"Now, hold on there, Matt," said the sheriff, stepping forward to greet the entourage. "We're going to get that thief and killer hung right on time just like I promised."

"See that you do," Thurston growled. "Because if you don't, you're going to be sorry you was ever born'd. I got you that star and I can take it away."

Even from a distance, Jake could see the sheriff cower under Thurston's attack. There would be no help from the local law. Miguel was being railroaded to a grisly death for the sole purpose of satisfying the bloodlust of a land baron. One thing was certain: If Alicia's brother was to be saved from the hangman's noose, it was going to be up to Jake to do it.

Chapter Two

As Jake watched the Thurston outfit head *en masse* toward one of the saloons, an idea started to form. After their long ride, they'd want to wet their trail-dry throats with whiskey. Maybe get something to eat too. That should give him enough time. He ducked back inside the livery stable and began to implement his plan.

First off, he heated some water and scraped the stubble from his face. Next, he washed up and combed his hair. He finished with fresh clothes from his saddlebag, the dressiest he had. Now, he'd see if he could pass for a hangman, one who was so eager to do his job right that he'd arrived early. Chances were, the sheriff wouldn't know the real one personally. If it turned out he did, Jake would simply claim to have taken his place. There was no telegraph in town so his story couldn't be checked.

He slid the Colt .44 out of its holster, broke it open,

and added another bullet to the chamber that he'd kept empty for safety. With all six chambers filled, he returned the weapon to its sheath. Then he stepped outside. The sheriff had disappeared.

Jake crossed the dusty street and walked down to the jail with what he hoped was an air of authority and purpose. Two old men stepped back to make room for him to pass. When he reached his destination, he took a deep breath and went inside. The sheriff heard his step and turned to stare with eyes that were filled with suspicion.

"What is it you want?" he asked, his tone unfriendly.

"I believe you requested my services," said Jake, nodding toward the gallows outside.

"Oh, yeah. It's about time you got here, Mullins. I was beginning to think I'd have to do the job myself."

Jake's dislike for the man grew even more intense.

"Tsk, tsk," he replied. "Never let an amateur do a job that a professional can do so much better. I'm here, now, and I need to see the prisoner."

"What for? You'll be seeing him tomorrow morning bright and early. I guarantee it."

Jake had a ready answer.

"Look, if you want me to do the job the way it's supposed to be done, I'll see him now. I have to know what I'll be working with."

A deputy ambled in from the back room. He was an older man. He'd overheard and was glaring at Jake like he was vermin.

"Oh, all right," the sheriff conceded. "Walkenshaw, here, can take you back there. I've got work to do."

Jake figured that the bulk of Gillaspy's work would

be keeping an eye on the construction of the gallows and cozying up to Matt Thurston at the saloon.

As soon as he was gone, Deputy Walkenshaw made a point of ignoring Jake's presence. He walked around the room checking this and that, leaving him to stand there, hat in hand. Walkenshaw was older than the sheriff, with a tanned, sun-lined face and a thin body that moved in an awkward, disjointed way, reminding Jake of a scarecrow. When he'd finished, at last, he settled down to fiddle with some paperwork.

"I'm in a bit of a hurry," Jake prodded.

"You really like your work, don't you?" said Walkenshaw, giving him a venomous look.

"Not particularly. Now, if you'd just take me to the prisoner."

Walkenshaw sighed and put the papers down.

"Come on, then," he said, as he pulled a set of keys from the desk.

Jake followed him to the cells.

"That boy didn't do nothing," said Walkenshaw. "He simply had the misfortune of being the first one they come across. So now Thurston wants him dead. Even had one of his boys lie at the trial. That old man don't want to know that the Sandoval boy didn't do it. He just wants to see somebody hang."

Jake was surprised at his defense. It sounded like he'd found an ally, an unlikely one at that.

"You've got company, son," the deputy called out. "You might not want to see him, though."

Miguel turned. There were bruises all over his face and one eye was swollen shut. Gillaspy had beaten him.

Jake fought back his rage. As soon as Miguel saw him, he rushed to the bars in surprise and relief. Walkenshaw was quick to note his reaction. The deputy and Jake exchanged glances.

"Look, I didn't see nothin'," he said. "You do whatever you have to, stranger, but be careful. Sheriff Gillaspy has got that whole outfit behind him, and he'll probably find some others to go with 'em. You know how folks can be."

Jake nodded his thanks. "I'm much obliged to you for not tipping him off."

"If you aim to make a break for it, I'm on duty after midnight. Tie me up and get that boy out of here."

"Thanks, Russ," said Miguel. "I think you're the only one in this whole town who believes I'm innocent."

"Not anymore. Now you, Mr. Hangman, had better get your talking done and get out of here before Gillaspy takes the notion to come back and fire a bunch of questions at you. He's heard some about this Mullins you're supposed to be."

"I'll be quick about it," he promised.

As soon as the deputy was gone, Jake asked Miguel if he was all right.

"I'm sure not feeling my best, but at least I'm alive—for now."

"I intend to see that you stay that way. I'll be coming for you right after midnight. Be ready."

After seeing the results of the beating his young brother-in-law had taken, it required all the self-restraint he could muster to walk quietly past Sheriff Gillaspy on his way back to the livery stable. When he was safely inside, away from prying eyes, he checked his new Winchester rifle to make sure it was ready. He needed another saddle so that Miguel could ride the blood bay. He also needed spare mounts. After the jail-break, they'd be running hard, probably for a long time.

He heard the hostler come in.

"Town's filling up," said the fellow. "Biggest crowd in a long time."

"I noticed. By the way, did you hear what they did with the prisoner's horse?"

"Sure. Mr. Thurston took it. Said it belonged to him, now."

Jake muttered an oath under his breath.

"Why did you want to know?" asked the hostler.

"Curious, that's all. Mr. Thurston seems to have everything his own way around here, doesn't he."

"Might say that. I reckon he pretty much owns the town. Owns the local law, anyway. He says jump and Gillaspy asks how high."

"And the townsfolk go along with that?"

"No reason not to. No sense in inviting trouble when you don't have to."

That was an attitude he'd seen before. People didn't want to take any risk and speak up. As a result, inno-cents like Miguel got hung.

He leaned against the wall and watched the hostler curry a pretty iron-gray mare.

"I've got a ranch south of here," he said in what he hoped was a casual manner. "I'm always on the lookout for good horseflesh. Know of any around here for sale?"

"Might. In fact, I've got a couple of good horses, myself. Want to take a look?"

"Sure. May as well."

He led Jake to the pole corral behind the stable.

"This here sorrel is a good one," he said, pointing to a mahogany gelding. "Have to ask a lot for it, though. The other one's a good horse too. Lots of staying power. Traded for 'em both a while back."

The other horse was black with a white blaze. It was a gelding too. Jake went over and examined them.

"Maybe I could use 'em. Let's dicker a little."

He ended up buying both horses, along with a well-used saddle.

Next he went to the general merchandise store and picked up a can of coffee, a couple of cans of peaches, bacon, and flour. He added two canteens, extra blankets, and a gray waterproof poncho that wouldn't show up from a distance. He looked for a coat for Miguel, but they didn't have any. Back at the livery, he packed the things away. While he was doing this, he pulled from a saddlebag an old pistol that had belonged to his Uncle Nate. The gun had been cleaned before he left the ranch. He loaded it and stuck it in his belt. Miguel would need a weapon.

When he'd finished preparing, there was nothing to do but watch and wait. At the tail end of daylight, he went down the street to a small café and ordered a bowl of stew. Walkenshaw sat at the other end of the room, eating pie and drinking coffee. They ignored each other. On his way back, he noticed that the saloons were filling to capacity for the evening's revelry. It seemed a hanging was good for business.

The hostler finished up his chores and went home.

He was replaced by a kid who slept there at night. As soon as the kid turned in, Jake struck a match to a lantern and saddled his horses. Then he put the two mounts he'd just bought on lead ropes. When this was done, he snuffed the lantern and went outside to watch the street. Noise and light spilled from all three saloons. Everything else was shut down and dark, except for the jail. There, a stream of lamplight escaped from the shutters.

While Jake watched, he saw another of Gillaspy's deputies making his evening rounds. Piedmont evidently had no town marshal. Probably Thurston didn't see the need for one since he was calling the shots. He wondered where the land baron and his outfit had gone. Probably turned in early, he decided. They'd want to be fresh for the morning's entertainment.

Minutes dragged slowly and turned into hours. Jake looked up at a sky that was sprinkled with stars. The Big Dipper, so familiar to him, was standing upright on its bowl, to the left of the North Star. It was ten o'clock. Two hours until midnight. A light wind swept across the arid land, raising the dirt in the street and sweeping it against the buildings. As usual in the desert, it had turned cold after sundown. He shrugged into the warmth of his duster. An hour passed, and part of another. It was almost time. He went in and brought the horses out. With one swift motion, he pulled the right side of his duster back away from his holster, making the .44 readily accessible. Then he waited quietly in the shadows for Walkenshaw to replace the deputy on duty. The sickle moon provided scant light to see by. But when they made their escape, darkness would be an asset. Soon the outline of a scarecrow made its way across the street. It avoided the scaffolding and entered the jail. The other deputy came out, mounted his horse, and headed east.

It was time. He climbed on the dun and rode across the street, leading the other horses. There he entered an alley that led to the back of the jail. Quietly, he fastened the reins to one of the bars and went in through the side door.

Walkenshaw looked up. "Been expecting you. Tie me up before you do anything."

Jake did so, quickly and efficiently. "You're a good man," he said.

"You just get that boy out of here and don't let them cutthroats kill either of you. I put the key on that hook over there."

Jake grabbed it and ran to the cell. Miguel was waiting. When the door swung open, he lunged into the corridor.

"*Gracias, mi amigo,*" Miguel said to Walkenshaw as they headed for the door.

"Wait a minute," called the deputy. "You'd better gag me or else give me a black eye so I can pretend I was knocked out."

Jake went over and pulled the bandanna from Walkenshaw's throat. It took only seconds to gag him.

Outside, he paused to listen. The only sounds came from the saloons, a mixture of music and raucous laughter. They mounted up. Jake grabbed the lead rope. Making as little noise as possible, they rode out of Piedmont.

Once they were outside of town, they spurred the horses and put as much distance as they could behind them.

"How much time do you think we have?" asked Miguel.

"Until somebody finds Deputy Walkenshaw, and I don't expect he'll be attracting any attention."

"That could be thirty minutes before dawn or five minutes after we left."

"We'd better hope that it's closer to dawn. You can bet they'll be trailing us like a swarm of mad hornets."

Jake reached back to the blankets that were tied behind his cantle. "Here," he said, taking one and tossing it to Miguel. "Put this around you. It's cold out tonight."

The boy draped it around his shoulders like a shawl.

"Jake, do you mind telling me where we're headed?"

"Toward the mountains. It'll be harder to find us there. If they catch up to us, we might be able to hold them off."

Miguel was silent for a while before saying what was on his mind.

"Nobody was happier to escape the noose than me, Jake. But as long as old man Thurston lives we're going to be on the run."

"Maybe we can find out who really killed his son."

"He wouldn't believe it if you gave him gold-plated proof. He doesn't want to hang the killer. He wants to hang me."

What Thurston didn't want, Jake decided, was to be proven wrong in front of an entire town. He didn't want to be caught looking like the arrogant, bull-headed fool that he was. Jake figured that if necessary to save face, the patriarch of the clan wouldn't hesitate to let the real killer go free and hang an innocent man in his place. He was the kind that Arizona could do without.

Jake was alert, wary of any movement or sound. To the south and east of Piedmont, he spotted the red glow of flames against the night sky.

"Look over your right shoulder, Miguel."

"*Madre de Dios,* a ranch has been torched."

Jake got a sick feeling in the pit of his stomach.

"Apaches. We'd better get as far away as we can, and pray hard that they don't cross our path."

"I didn't know that Apaches fought at night," said Miguel. "Don't they believe that their spirits will wander forever if they get killed after dark?"

"Yes," said Jake, "and ordinarily it's true that they won't attack at night, but they're plenty mad since the Camp Grant massacre where so many of their people were murdered. There wasn't any sense in what was done."

"Well, the Apaches weren't taking much of a risk tonight," said Miguel. "No one at that ranch would have been expecting a nighttime attack. Especially since the famous General Crook has arrived to settle the Apache wars."

In Jake's opinion, Crook's presence tended to give folks a false sense of security. After all, Arizona Territory was a big place to patrol. He and Miguel rode with care.

By the time a blush of orange-pink was visible over the mountains, they were miles away from Piedmont and its gallows. When the sun had cleared the horizon, they paused long enough to change horses and refresh themselves. The past couple of days with little sleep were taking their toll on Jake.

"Had you not come along, I'd be dead by now," said Miguel, whose execution had been scheduled for shortly after dawn. Jake noticed an involuntary shudder shake the boy's shoulders.

"What are brothers for?" he said.

"How did you know to come to Piedmont?"

"I've been following your trail for weeks on Alicia's orders. That I arrived in time was pure luck."

"Or my sister's prayers."

"That too."

"Well, *gracias.* I owe you and Walkenshaw my life. At least what's left of it."

Jake intended to see that Miguel stayed alive, and that he got safely back to his sister. But with Apaches to the south and a posse from the east, it was a job that wouldn't shape up to be easy.

Chapter Three

The sun was halfway to its zenith when Jake saw the dusty settlement up ahead. The village consisted of a dozen or more adobes that were huddled together, plus a number of outbuildings of different sizes. Set off from the rest of the village was a larger structure. Even from a distance, it was easy to see the tall crucifix that stood in front, carved from wood by a man who knew his craft. Although man-made, the buildings appeared to blend into the landscape as if they were a natural part of it.

When he and Miguel reached the edge, they rode in slowly. Strings of colorful red peppers hung from the vigas of the buff-colored dwellings. Nearby, a blind-folded burro plodded around an arristra, grinding wheat into flour. The village was rich in children, all of whom stopped their play in order to stare at the strangers.

"*Buenos dias,*" said Miguel.

"*Buenos dias,*" replied a dark-eyed boy of about eleven

who appeared to be the leader. "I will get my grandfather."

Leaving his playmates, he ran to one of the houses. Shortly, he returned with a man whose dark hair was liberally sprinkled with gray. Jake noticed the pistol that was stuck in his belt. A woman appeared in one of the doorways. She, too, was armed. While the man and boy approached, a second boy ran off in the other direction. No doubt he'd gone to spread the alarm and bring in the men of the settlement.

"How may I be of service, señores?" asked the elder. His eyes had a look of shrewdness, and though advanced in years, his posture was ramrod straight.

"All we need is a place to rest for a brief time and to water our horses," said Jake.

The patriarch of the village looked them over. "Trouble follows you, no?"

Jake felt he owed the man the truth.

"Most certainly it does, or it will."

"You are running from the law?"

Jake and his brother-in-law exchanged glances.

"In a way," he admitted. "My young friend, here, was about to be hung for a murder he didn't commit, and for stealing money that he didn't take. I saw no justice in that."

The man glanced at Miguel's bruised and swollen face. Then he looked hard at Jake as if he were attempting to read his soul.

"Nor do I see justice in that," he said finally. "Now, tell me, señor, how did this come about?"

"It was the doings of a land baron named Matt

Thurston. Because Miguel was the first man they spotted after a robbery and murder they decided he was guilty. It counted for nothing that he didn't have the stolen money, or that he proclaimed his innocence. Thurston wanted blood. The so-called trial was a farce. The judge was drunk."

The old man nodded. "Yes. I have heard much of this Thurston hombre. He is *muy mal*. Very bad. He takes what he wants and does what he pleases. This is no way for a man of honor to live."

"I doubt if anyone has ever accused Matt Thurston of having honor," said Miguel. "That so-called sheriff he's bought and paid for is short on it too."

The old man looked again at Miguel's face and appeared to reach a decision.

"My name is Eduardo Santos and you are welcome to our village."

At that moment, more than a dozen armed men appeared from a shallow arroyo that backed the small community. Santos waved them off.

"It is all right. These men are our guests."

Jake breathed a sigh of relief. He would not like to have Santos and the villagers for enemies.

The children, who'd been quietly watching, went back to their play, while he and Miguel were ushered into Santos' house. Here they were served beans and venison wrapped in tortillas by señora Santos, a grandmotherly woman with a pleasant smile. When they'd finished eating, their host engaged them in conversation.

"Amigo, which one of Thurston's men were you supposed to have killed?" he asked, addressing Miguel.

"Wade Thurston, his son."

Santos' look was one of surprise and concern.

"I know this man's reputation. One of his hired hands he would readily forget. But he will avenge his son. He won't stop until he hunts you down, or until you kill him. It will be one or the other. I'm afraid you must not linger. If he were to discover that we are giving you sanctuary, he would try to destroy us. My people are my responsibility, and I have the children to think of."

"We understand," said Jake. "We want no harm to come to you. As soon as our horses are watered and fed, we'll be moving on."

A look of relief crossed Santos' weathered face.

"If they come, we will tell them we haven't seen you. A necessary lie. I'll have my sons go and wipe out your tracks that led here. If you can avoid Apaches, the mountains will give you better shelter than our village. However, there is also a place not far from here. It is owned by a rancher named Klaus Gebhardt."

"Under the circumstances," said Jake, "I doubt if Gebhardt would welcome us, either."

"Perhaps you are wrong. He has much dislike for Thurston. One of his ranch hands was beaten almost to death by his four sons. He would like to see this scoundrel get his 'comeuppance.' I believe that's the way señor Gebhardt put it."

"Then maybe we'll pay him a visit," said Jake.

He turned to the woman. "*Gracias,* señora, for the fine meal."

"*De nada,*" she replied.

"Señor Santos, we'll see about our horses and be on our way."

Within the hour, they'd put the village far behind them. Jake was weary and in need of rest. It was obvious that Miguel was, too, but rest would have to wait. Thankfully, there was still no sign of Thurston's posse.

They rode hard, stopping once to switch to fresh mounts. When they came to a draw, they reined up. It wasn't deep, but it would be enough to shelter them from the eyes of anyone up on the flat.

"We'll camp here for a while," said Jake. "If you'll keep watch while I get a little sleep, I'll do the same for you. Wake me if you see or hear anything."

Jake spread out his blankets and quickly dropped off. He wasn't sure how long he'd slept before Miguel was shaking his shoulder.

"Get up," said his brother-in-law. "Someone is coming."

Jake was suddenly wide awake. "How many?" he asked.

"Only one, but he's coming from the direction of Piedmont."

Silently Jake cursed his bad luck. Then it occurred to him that Gillaspy wouldn't have sent a lone man to hunt them down. Curious as to who it was, he scrambled to the top of the draw and looked out over the valley. A single rider appeared to be following their trail. He was astride a fine-looking horse and had another equally fine-looking horse on a lead rope.

"Could that be one of the Thurstons?" said Miguel.

"All we have to do is wait awhile in order to find out."

When the man drew closer, Jake recognized him. He blinked his eyes in disbelief.

"It's Decker," he said.

"It can't be," said Miguel. "Why is he out here, so far from Prescott? And why is he following us?"

"In a few minutes, we'll ask him."

A couple of years earlier, Jake had rescued Ryan Decker from the desert after he'd been robbed and left to die by the outlaw Culebra and his gang. He'd befriended the young man and made him a partner in a treasure hunt. But the last he'd heard, Decker had gone home to his grandfather who was a judge in Prescott. There, he'd gotten a job working for a newspaper called the *Miner*.

Decker slowed when he saw that their tracks led to the draw. He reined up and swung down from the saddle. Although he was only a few years younger than Jake, he still had his boyish good looks, the kind that attracted young ladies.

"Well, come on in, amigo," said Jake, showing his head and shoulders above the rim. "Don't dally there all day."

Decker grinned and led his horses forward.

"Am I glad to see you two."

He took one look at Miguel's bruised and swollen face and grimaced.

"The work of Sheriff Gillaspy, no doubt."

"Him and one of the Thurstons," Miguel admitted. "Ben to be exact. And what do you know about my troubles?"

"I passed through Piedmont and heard a lot of talk."

"What are you doing so far from home?" said Jake. "Why aren't you still in Prescott where you belong?"

Decker gave him a sheepish grin. "Well, I kind of lost my job. You see, the editor is real strong-minded about certain things and we had a whopper of a disagreement. Being the boss, he always wins arguments. So, at his suggestion, we parted company. I packed my things and headed for your ranch. But when I got there, I found Alicia upset. She said that Miguel had flown the nest and that she'd sent you after him. She's worried sick."

"And so you told her you'd be glad to pick up my trail, track me down, and tell me to get myself home," said Jake. "Preferably with Miguel in tow."

"That's about the size of it," he agreed. "I came directly north, avoiding some of the stops you must have made, so I gained on you. But I never dreamed that I'd find that gallows in Piedmont with Miguel's name on it."

"You must have come through right after we made our break."

"Yep. I camped near town and got there just at dawn."

He glanced at Miguel. "I gotta tell you, you're not popular, amigo. You cheated those folks out of a hanging. But I have to say that I'm glad you did."

"You didn't happen to run into a posse?" said Jake.

"No. Right after you broke jail, there was an Apache attack at a ranch south of town. All of the men are armed and on watch in case the renegades head north. It's bought you some time. The more they delay, the colder your trail is going to be. I took out right after I learned what had happened."

"I didn't rob and kill that man," said Miguel.

Decker shoved his hat to the back of his head. "Don't need to tell me. I've known you too long."

"You've done some hard riding to catch up," said Jake. "We stopped at that Mexican village and they fed us and gave us a chance to care for our horses. But we couldn't have been there more'n a couple of hours."

"You've been asleep for quite a while," said Miguel.

"I saw the village in the distance." said Decker. "A couple of men who appeared to be villagers were wiping out your tracks. I figured you'd head for the mountains, so I stayed clear of the settlement and soon picked up your trail again."

"Santos, the old man in charge, helped us all he could," said Jake. "It was likely his sons that you saw."

Decker dropped the reins and took a swig from his canteen. Jake was impressed at how he'd grown from a green kid to a seasoned Westerner in the time that he'd known him.

"I wasn't in Piedmont for long," said Decker, capping the canteen, "but long enough to hear that old man Thurston is fit to be tied. It seems that none of the men would leave their families after the Apache attack to form a posse. To their way of thinking, their families came first. The sheriff and his deputies refused to ride out with him too. Even his own hands were reluctant. But I expect the old man is going to rant and rave and throw his weight around until he finally gets his way."

Jake figured he was right. They'd had a bit of luck, but it wasn't apt to last. Not with so much hate and bloodlust spurring the head of the clan.

"Are we going to that ranch señor Santos told us about?" asked Miguel.

"I kinda figured on it."

"What ranch?" asked Decker.

"One that's not far from here. It's owned by a man named Gebhardt. Seems he's got no liking for Thurston, either."

"Think we can hole up there for a while?"

"I don't know. At least we can tell our story. The more who know the truth of what happened, the better. Reckon it's best we head for the mountains anyway.

Jake knew they could lose themselves in the high country. There would be water and game, and places to hide. Truth be told, though, he longed for home. It had been weeks since he'd seen Alicia and the baby. What's more, he didn't like leaving the ranch so long in the hands of his foreman. If Miguel had only stayed where he belonged instead of wandering off in search of adventure, none of this would have happened. He hoped Miguel was getting his fill.

The three men saddled up and headed toward the ranch of Klaus Gebhardt. It was late in the day when they approached it. Like Santos' village, it was the color of earth and blended into the landscape. The main house was a sprawling affair, larger, even, than the house Jake had built for Alicia.

Before they were able to get close, they were intercepted. Five of Gebhardt's hands came riding up to them, blocking their way.

"Uh-oh," said Decker. "Looks like the welcoming committee."

"Have you got business here?" asked a rough-looking hombre with a broken nose. He had a scar above his left eye and a couple of front teeth were missing.

"Yes," said Jake. "We want to talk to your boss, Mr. Gebhardt."

"If you're looking for jobs, we don't need any more help so you can just ride on."

"That's not the nature of our business."

"Then just what is the nature of your business?"

"I'll discuss that with Mr. Gebhardt when I see him." Broken nose didn't like the answer.

"Bart, you'd better go tell the boss," said an older fellow. "It might be that he'd want to talk to these fellows."

Bart appeared to think it over.

"All right," he said finally. "But if the boss says to get lost, the three of you are riding out of here."

"You might tell him that I'm Matt Thurston's worst enemy," said Jake.

Bart's expression changed from one of hostility to one of interest.

"That ain't so, mister. I know it for a fact 'cause I'm Thurston's worst enemy."

Jake recalled the story that Santos had told.

"You must be the one that his boys jumped a while back."

"So you heard. Yep, I'm the one, and I'd be right pleased to repay 'em for what they done. Come on to the house."

A servant ushered them into a large room where Jake caught the scent of crushed herbs. The room contained four hide-covered chairs and a big Spanish cupboard with detailed carving on the front. A large portion of one wall was decorated by a colorful woven tapestry depicting a scene in mythology. Everything there bespoke of wealth and good taste.

It turned out that Klaus Gebhardt was a man in his mid-thirties. He had blond hair, cold blue eyes, and sun-reddened skin. His bearing was military. From the looks of him, he wasn't the kind of man that anyone would want to cross.

"This fellow claims to be Thurston's worst enemy," said Bart. "He wants to talk to you about something."

"Thank you Tidwell, that will be all," said Gebhardt speaking with a slight German accent.

As soon as Tidwell and the man-servant had gone, Gebhardt appraised the strangers. Jake introduced himself and his partners.

"Please be seated," he invited.

Gebhardt went over to the cupboard and took out a fancy cut-glass decanter of whiskey, along with some glasses.

"May I pour you gentlemen a drink?"

Miguel declined, but Jake and Decker accepted the crystal glasses of amber liquid.

"Now, what is all this about Matt Thurston?" he asked, seating himself in a large chair across from them.

Briefly, Jake related the events that had brought them to his ranch.

"Thurston and those sons of his are beneath contempt," said Gebhardt when Jake had finished. "Some of his men are too. Not to mention that he owns that pompous sheriff who passes for the law in Piedmont. It's time he was taken down a few notches."

It seemed to Jake that, at least in sentiment, Gebhardt was an ally.

"Señor Santos told us about Thurston's sons beating up one of your hands," he said. "I take it that hand was Bart Tidwell."

"Yes. Tidwell is hungry for revenge. I can't say that I blame him."

"Sir, what do you think the chances are of getting a deputy federal marshal in here to investigate?" asked Decker.

Gebhardt grimaced. "I'd say they're about the same as getting Her Majesty, Queen Victoria, to stop by for tea."

Jake considered the remoteness of the place and the shortage of deputies and figured he was right.

"Well, we all agree that something's got to be done," he said. "Up to now, I've been wholly concerned with keeping Miguel's neck out of Sheriff Gillaspy's noose. But maybe it's time to go on the offensive."

"You're probably right," said Gebhardt. "Still, there must be planning and caution. Otherwise, all will be lost."

"Maybe one of us could infiltrate Thurston's place," said Decker. "Find out what they know about the shooting."

"That isn't a bad idea," said Gebhardt, "but unfortunately Thurston knows Tidwell, and almost everyone around here, on sight. He certainly knows young Sandoval. What about you, Mr. Decker?"

"No," said Jake. "It's too dangerous to try something like that. We need to go at this in a different way."

"I notice you're a little undermanned," said the German. "When you decide what you're going to do, I'll send Tidwell with you. He almost died at their hands and he wants to remind them."

"Well, I can't say how good our chances are, but if he's willing to come along, he's welcome."

Gebhardt set his glass on a small chair-side table and looked Jake in the eye. "I'm sure you realize that you will remain hunted men until they hang you or shoot you. Your only recourse is to remove the threat. My father, who was a military man, advised that the best defense is a strong attack."

Jake took a swallow of whiskey before answering.

"I expect your father was right. It's just that I want to pick the time and I want to choose the place."

Gebhardt smiled, a smile that actually warmed his ice-blue eyes. "A wise decision and I wish you the best of fortune."

Santos had been right. Gebhardt was an ally. Jake lifted his glass.

"Here's to success," he said.

"To success," Gebhardt responded.

Outside, again, they invited Tidwell to join them.

"Is it all right with you, boss?" he asked.

"Yes. I offered them your services."

"Good. It's time I got to pay them no-accounts back for what they done to me."

He turned to Jake. "What do we do? Head for the mountains and wait for them to come after us?"

"We've not got much choice," said Jake. "They're on the attack. Up there, I can make it cost them."

"Take two of the best horses," said Gebhardt. "I trust you've got plenty of ammunition. Get some supplies from the cook."

When they were ready to pull out, Gebhardt shook Jake's hand.

"Thurston and his gang of vigilantes are sure to come here. I'll do what I can to stall and mislead them."

"Anything you can do will be appreciated."

With that, four men left the K/G hacienda and made their way toward the sanctuary of the high country. It was late. A cold wind blew down from the northern peaks, the three of them making up a sacred mountain of the Navajo. But Jake and the others were headed eastward. Miguel had Decker's spare coat. A good thing. It would be even colder on the mountain.

Chapter Four

Matt Thurston stomped out of the jail, the rowels on his spurs jingling on impact. Fury etched his harsh, weathered face. Like the parting of the Red Sea, the crowd of bystanders made way for him to pass through. They'd come to watch a hanging and the prisoner was gone.

Thurston's nephew, Roger Byrd, came running up to him. Scrawny, pale, and awkward, he was called Birdie by everyone who knew him.

"I just heard, Uncle Matt," he said, panting for breath. "Is it really true that Sandoval broke out of jail?"

Thurston glared at him. "It's true enough. Though it's beyond me how Gillaspy allowed him to do it."

Birdie eyed the vacant scaffold. "Was he alone?"

"No, he had help. Some fellow came in, armed to the teeth, and busted him out."

"Who?"

"How in blazes would I know? That sorry excuse for a deputy let himself get captured and tied up. Wouldn't be surprised if he was sleeping when it happened. I knew better than to trust Gillaspy to get the job done. He should have stayed with the prisoner himself, instead of leaving everything to his flunky."

"Are you going after Sandoval?"

"You can bet your life on it. Just as soon as I get the boys rounded up. Where are they, anyway? They was supposed to be here to watch the hangin'."

"They're close by. They stopped on the way to get some breakfast."

Thurston made a sound of disgust. "Ain't that just like 'em. Always thinking about their bellies."

"I'll run get 'em for you."

"You do that. That coward Gillaspy refuses to form a posse. Says the men of the town won't leave their families what with that Injun attack so close. It's going to be up to us."

"I'll hurry 'em fast as I can."

Thurston watched the scrawny son of his sister running down the boardwalk, pushing his way through the crowd that lingered. He felt a sense of irritation. Why couldn't Birdie be more like his own sons, he wondered. Shrugging, he turned his attention to the more important matter of catching Wade's killer.

Another half hour passed before they met at the livery stable. His remaining sons, Thad, Gabe, and Ben were there. The boys looked enough alike, and like himself, that no one could doubt they were related. Then there was his foreman, Sam Conrad, high-strung as a coon dog right before a hunt. Last, there was Birdie, for what little he was worth.

Supplies had been hurriedly packed in panniers. More ammunition had been purchased and extra mounts secured. Thurston hoped it wouldn't take long to run the young whelp, and whoever was with him, to ground. Still, he aimed to stay with it until the job was done.

"We're ready, boss," said Conrad.

"Then let's get shut of this town."

"We ain't been deputized yet," said Thad. "Hadn't we better go get Gillaspy to swear us in?"

Thurston grabbed the reins of his horse. "To blazes with Gillaspy. We don't need no tin star to take care of that killer. All we need is a .44 and a length of hemp."

With that said, he stepped into the stirrup and led the way. As they rode out of town, they had an audience. He noticed that Conrad enjoyed the attention. His foreman was ordinary in every way, and on his own, nobody would give him a second glance. Thurston, himself, didn't have that trouble. He'd learned long ago that it was good to make people sit up and take notice. He usually enjoyed it. But today it brought him no pleasure. Not with Wade so newly buried. Wade had been the smartest of his offspring, the one he'd trusted the most. This was the reason the boy had been put in charge of the cash that was stolen. It pained him that his trust was what had gotten his son murdered. The whereabouts of that money remained a mystery. Only the killer knew where it was hidden, and Gillaspy hadn't been able to beat it out of him.

The trail they followed angled to the northeast. The

robbery and shooting had occurred to the south and west of Piedmont. It appeared that Sandoval and his pal weren't headed back to retrieve the loot. At least not right away. No matter, he thought, once the killer was caught, he'd be more than happy to talk. He'd tell where that money was hid or he'd be skinned alive. Thurston had found that a sharp skinning knife always brought the tongue-tied around. He'd learned that on the Boston waterfront where he'd survived his childhood.

It was easy to tell by the tracks that two riders were leading spare mounts. Those extra horses meant they could go farther and faster. Not good. He grudgingly admitted that whoever had planned the jailbreak had done it well.

While they followed the trail, he and his sons kept alert for Apaches. The lightning raid on that ranch was unexpected and ill timed as far as Thurston was concerned. Afterward, those raiders had disappeared like mist in the sunshine. But who knew how far they'd gone, or for how long.

No doubt, a lot of the Indian trouble they were having now was due to the fools that took part in the Camp Grant massacre. Fools that went by the name of the Tucson Committee of Public Safety, along with some others who were just as bad. In April they'd made a surprise attack on the camp and killed a hundred Apaches, many of 'em squaws and kids. "Purely murder," President Grant had said. Well, them Apaches was getting back. Revenge—it was a raw need. He knew all about it.

When they came, at last, to a creek edged by paloverde

and creosote brush, they crossed at the place where their quarry had crossed. But on the far side, all sign of them mysteriously disappeared.

"What in blazes!" said Thurston, venting his anger. "I don't believe this. Get down off that horse, Conrad, and take a closer look."

Conrad was the best tracker among them. He walked up and down the creek bank and then ranged farther out. After a time, he shook his head.

"They've wiped out their sign real good. Could be they rode on up the creek. If so, they went a long way."

Frustrated, and driven by cold fury, he ordered them forward. "They're trying to throw us off. We'll keep riding in the same direction. I'm betting we'll pick up their trail again."

"But if we can't see their tracks," said Thad, "what happened to 'em?"

Thad was the dimmest of all his boys. He was nothing like Wade and he could surely try a man's patience.

"They started covering their tracks. That's what happened to 'em. Just keep on going. We'll find 'em."

He recalled a Mexican village not far distant. It occurred to him that Sandoval might have friends in that settlement who would give him refuge. The more he thought about it, the more convinced he became that this was so. He promised himself that if they didn't turn his boy's killer over on demand, he would tear the place apart. Once he had Sandoval again, he'd burn the place down. Teach 'em to harbor killers. He told the others what he had in mind.

"What if they shoot at us, Pa?" said Thad.

"We'll put the scare in 'em right off. They won't dare. They'll be begging us to take that killer and his pal."

"Then we're going to haul 'em back to town and get 'em hung, ain't we, Pa?"

"Shut up!" said Ben. "I'm tired of listening to you."

"We ain't taking 'em back," said Thurston. "I'm going to find out what Sandoval did with our money. Then I'm going to hang him myself. That other one too."

The thought of vengeance eased him some. When he spotted the cluster of adobes he stood in his stirrups in order to get a better look. To his surprise, the place appeared deserted.

"Ride in careful-like," he warned. "They might be hid out, watching for us."

When they entered the ghostly village, the only ones in sight were two flea-bag mongrels and one old man. The dogs barked until the old man ordered them to be quiet. He held a hoe in one hand for he'd been tending what was left of a vegetable patch.

"Hey, there!" Thurston called.

The old man looked at him.

"Señores, how may I serve you?"

"You can tell me where you've got that Mex killer hid out, and his amigo too."

"I'm afraid I do not understand. We have no killers here."

Thurston's patience was at an end. He drew his pistol and fired. The bullet plowed dirt inches from the old man's foot. The man winced, yet stood his ground.

"Now, you listen to me," said Thurston. "If you don't

tell me what I want to know, the next bullet is going to go right through your heart."

"No, señor, the next will go through yours. Holster your gun."

Thurston nearly swallowed his wad of tobacco when the heads and shoulders of a dozen or more men appeared above the ditch that ran along the back of the village. Their guns were pointed straight at him and his boys. If they decided to cut loose, it would be a slaughter. Thurston started backing down.

"Now, hold on a minute," he said, easing his gun back into its holster. "I can see this has all been a misunderstanding. We was out looking for a fellow named Sandoval and his partner, and we thought they might have come here. Seein' as how we was mistaken, we'll just ride off peaceful-like."

The old man smiled. "Of course, you made a mistake, señor. A bad one. Leave our village at once and don't return. Should you do so, I assure you your welcome will be a warm one. We will send all of you to straight to purgatory."

"Let's get out of here," said Conrad under his breath.

Warily, they backed their horses away. Then they wheeled and rode off at a gallop. When they'd put some distance between themselves and the armed villagers, Thurston gave the signal to stop.

"Are we heading home now, Pa?" asked Thad. "That was a close one."

"No." There was no way he was going to quit. "We'll keep on going. When it gets dark we'll make camp and try to pick up their trail again in the morning. I'm going to send one of you boys back to keep an eye on that village. See if they're hiding Sandoval there. I don't trust 'em and I owe 'em for the way they done me just now."

"I'll go," Thad volunteered.

He was eager. Thurston would give his youngest son that. But he was the last person for such a job.

"No. You're coming with us. I'm sending Ben."

Thad started to protest and then thought better of it.

"Is there anyplace close to the village where they might have gone?" asked Gabe, the tallest, best-looking of his brood.

Thurston thought about it. "There's a ranch. Remember that fellow you and your brothers taught a lesson a while back? Name was Tidwell."

"I remember."

"Well, he works at that ranch for a fellow named Klaus Gebhardt."

"I've seen him," said Ben. "German fellow, ain't he?"

"Maybe. Anyway, he had words with Gillaspy about us. Mostly complaints and threats. But I noticed that he didn't come after us, himself, which means he's a little yellow and a lot smart."

"Might ought to have a look at his place," said Conrad, who'd been listening to the exchange.

"Yeah, that's what I was thinking," said Thurston. "Gebhardt hates us like poison. It'd be just like him to give refuge to Sandoval and his partner."

"But he'll have a lot of men working for him," said Gabe. "We'll be outnumbered and outgunned."

Thurston threw him a look of disgust.

"I don't aim for us to go riding up to the front gate in

broad daylight. We'll split up. Watch from a distance. See if Sandoval and his partner are there. Then, come nightfall, we'll sneak in and capture the two of 'em."

"Since you're planning on hitting Gebhardt's place," said Conrad, "it seems to me we ought to keep Ben with us. He's a good shot and he's got nerve."

Thurston watched Ben puff up under the praise. Of his three remaining sons, Ben was the smartest and toughest. He could understand Conrad's wanting him along.

"Look," he said. "I can't take a chance. We don't know where they're hiding. Some of them villagers might be Sandoval's friends. Relatives, even. Ben is the best one to keep watch and let us know."

Conrad grudgingly agreed. They both knew that neither Birdie nor Thad were capable. And even Gabe wasn't as good a choice as Ben.

Thurston watched as his son turned and headed back toward the village. Then he nudged his mount forward.

It was almost dark when they stopped and made camp in a shallow wash that for a time, at least, was dry. The sides gave them protection from the cold night winds that warned of an early winter. It also hid the small fire they built for their coffee and bacon. Short rations at best, but they warmed the insides.

"You take the first watch, Thad," he ordered. "Gabe and Birdie can spell you."

"Oh, Pa, why does somebody have to keep watch, anyway?" Thad complained. "We're the ones that's doing the hunting."

Thurston sprang like a mountain cat and backhanded him. The report was sharp and Thad toppled on his hind side. Blood dribbled from one corner of his mouth and there was fear and hurt in his eyes.

"Look, boy, when I tell you to do something, you do it. There's Apaches about, for one thing. Not to mention that those men at the village might decide to come after us. And there's another thing to remember: The hunted can turn into hunters."

Without another word, Thad wiped his mouth, hefted his rifle, and took up his post. The rest of them climbed into their bedrolls.

When Thurston hauled himself out of his blankets, the sky had lightened from black to a smoky gray. He took a deep breath of cold desert air and pulled on his boots. He saw that Gabe was on watch.

"No trouble?" he asked.

"Nope. It was downright peaceful."

Thurston went over and none too gently nudged the sleeping bodies with the toe of his boot. Grumbling, Conrad, Thad, and Birdie crawled out of their beds. After the quickest and skimpiest of meals, they were ready to ride.

When the sun made its appearance over the mountaintop, it brought light to an arid landscape of cholla, yuccas, and mesquite. Here and there, the desert was dotted with clumps of brittlebush. This was where Thurston felt most at home. The Boston slums of his youth were but faded, unhappy memories. The sun had climbed by the time they reached the ridge that overlooked the Gebhardt ranch.

"Stay back here," he ordered, pulling a pair of field glasses from one of his saddlebags. "I'm going up to spy the place out."

He cat-hopped the *grullo* up the steep slope. A dozen yards from the top he dismounted, not wanting to skyline himself. From there, he made his way on foot. His bulk was a handicap for such unaccustomed exertion and he panted for air. As he approached the top, he dropped and crawled to the edge. What he saw below impressed him, and he wasn't easily impressed. Besides numerous outbuildings, there was a big corral and a barn. But they all played second fiddle to the main house—a large, sprawling adobe that could brag of an inner courtyard and a heavily carved front door. He felt a pang of envy. It made his own place seem small and shabby by comparison, a fact that caused him to dislike the German all the more.

He wondered if Gebhardt had a woman. Women were often a man's vulnerability. Not his, of course. After a couple years of marriage, Viola had lost her looks. As time went by, she meant less and less to him. Toward the end of her life, he barely tolerated her. She'd been gone for years, now, and he rarely thought of her. But he knew that with other men, and with other women, it was often different.

As he watched, two cowhands headed from the bunkhouse to the corral. They saddled a couple of paints from the remuda and rode off. Over to the right, a thin wisp of smoke wafted from the cookhouse chimney. A door swung open and a man appeared and shook out a towel. Probably Gebhardt's man-servant. He groped for the word they were called. Then it came to him—valet.

He back-crawled from the edge and made his way down to the *grullo*. When he reached the others, they were waiting expectantly.

"Well, what did you see?" asked Conrad. "Are they down there?"

"Can't tell. Maybe."

"We could sneak in and grab 'em as soon as it gets dark," said Thad.

"I told you, I don't know if they're down there. But you're right. We'd best find out tonight."

Thurston cut off a chunk of chewing tobacco and put the rest of the plug away. He'd always been able to think better with a good chaw in his mouth.

"Then it's agreed," said Gabe. "We'll ride in there come nightfall."

Thurston thought about it for a minute.

"No," he said. "I've changed my mind. We won't wait 'til dark. We're going to ride in, neighborly like, and find out if that killer is there or if he's passed by. If he's still there, we'll order 'em to hand him over. Tell 'em we're the law. If he was there and left, we'll find out where he was headed."

"Aren't you afraid that Gebhardt might still be mad about what we did to his hired hand?" said Gabe.

Thurston shifted the tobacco wad to the other side of his jaw.

"What do I care? If that German wants to start trouble, we'll finish it for him. Besides, he's not going to want to get that fancy place of his all shot up. I know how his kind thinks."

Ignoring the skeptical look his foreman was giving him, Thurston mounted up. Gebhardt didn't know it, but he was about to get paid a social call.

Long before they got to the house, they were met by seven hard-faced men who sported revolvers.

"Was there something you wanted?" asked the one in charge. He was lean, almost gaunt, with sun-dried mahogany skin and eyes that seemed to look right through to the core.

"We're here to talk to your boss," said Thurston in his haughtiest manner. "I was told his name is Gebhardt."

"You can go ahead and tell me whatever it is you want to say to him. I'll see that Mr. Gebhardt hears it."

Thurston felt himself swell with rage. This wasn't the treatment he was accustomed to. Still, he couldn't afford to lose his temper. Not with all of those armed men facing him. A misstep now, and he could end up in a hole in the ground. He fixed the gaunt cowhand with a stare.

"Tell him we're here. Let him make up his own mind about seeing us."

The cowhand stared back. "As far as you're concerned, he already has. He's not seeing you. Now, turn around and ride off."

Thurston tried again.

"We're here on important business. We're after a killer named Sandoval. He shot my son and stole my money. There's another man with him who broke him out of the Piedmont jail. I'm prepared to offer a sizable reward."

Flanked by half a dozen others, Gebhardt's spokesman had the upper hand.

"I'm telling you for the last time, the boss has no interest in your money. He has no interest in this Sandoval. And he has no interest in you. Now go!"

"Come on," Conrad warned. "We can take this up later."

Frustrated for the second time in as many days, Thurston wheeled his mount and rode off. His sons followed with Birdie and Conrad beside them.

Thurston's thoughts were murderous. Had Gebhardt's men not been armed and expecting trouble, he'd have shot them from their saddles. The German would pay for his arrogance, he promised. And so would that Mexican village.

Chapter Five

Leaving Gebhardt's ranch behind, Jake and his three companions rode until dusk. As they were losing the light, they made camp near a river that nurtured ironwood trees and paloverde. Before the first streaks of dawn, they pulled out. Soon they were climbing into the foothills. The vegetation around them gradually changed. Piñons and cedars took the place of cactus and mesquite. On hearing their approach, a piglike javelina scurried into the brush. Always, they were alert for Apaches. Always, they watched their back trail for the posse.

"To my way of thinking," said Tidwell, "this is too much like we're running scared." There was an edge to his voice that bespoke a hot temper and an impatient nature.

"Of course we're running," said Jake. "But think of it this way. We're drawing the enemy to us."

Suggesting that this was merely a different approach seemed to appease Tidwell. Jake considered the man. He was far different from his fair-haired boss. Gebhardt played the aristocrat, a military one at that. He carefully considered every move before he made it. And always, he kept his emotions under rigid control. Tidwell, on the other hand, was impulsive. No doubt he'd lash out in anger or frustration. He bore a lot of scars that indicated his lack of restraint. Even though he was an ally, Jake was leery of trusting such a man too much, and figured he'd bear watching.

All day they rode. When they made camp that evening, they were in the pines. Jake chose a place that was backed by a bluff. The stone wall protected them from behind, while they had a clear view of the approaches from below.

"It's best that we make a cold camp," he said. "There's no sense in making it easy for Thurston, and we don't want to reveal our location to any Apache scout who might happen to be up this way."

"So now we wait," said Decker.

"Now we wait."

While the others bedded down in their blankets, Jake took the first watch. Positioned as they were between two enemies, they couldn't afford to be careless. In the distant west, the last colors of a glowing sunset fringed the horizon. Already the air was chill, and it would grow colder on the mountain as the night progressed. While he watched the Evening Star appear, he pictured Alicia so far away. He hoped she could sense that he was thinking of her and their child. He hoped he wouldn't fail her, and that, finally, he would be able to bring her the gift she wanted most—her brother.

Matt Thurston seethed with rage at the reception he'd gotten at the Gebhardt ranch. One day soon, he promised himself, he'd settle the score with that upstart German. His name was one on a growing list.

For a man accustomed to respect, and to getting his own way, Thurston was having a rough time. The trouble had begun with the jailbreak. Ever since Sandoval had gotten away from him, he'd met with nothing but insolence and failure. But this only strengthened his resolve.

Thad spoke up. "I don't like what we're doing, Pa."

"What don't you like about it, as if I cared?"

"Tracking down them two fellows. They're apt to be downright salty. I think we should have brung Ben along."

Before he could answer, Conrad reined up and swung down from his horse. He squatted on his haunches and surveyed the ground.

"This is their trail all right, boss. But it ain't the two of 'em anymore. There's four. And they've got twice as many horses. They're aimed straight ahead, toward the mountains, just like you had it figured."

Four men. Their number had doubled. Thurston didn't like it. He was only one ahead in manpower, now. That is if you counted Birdie for anything. He stared into the distance as if trying to spot them. The balance of power had shifted considerably. Still, his need for revenge gnawed at him, and he'd come too far to turn tail and run.

"Let's get on with it," he ordered.

All of a sudden he started to feel the excitement of the chase. Maybe it was because the odds were more even, and the challenge greater. Maybe it was the sense that they were, at last, closing in.

They'd covered a few more miles when Birdie sounded the alarm.

"We've got riders on our tail," he said.

Thurston turned in the saddle to have a look and muttered a curse.

"It's them cowhands from Gebhardt's ranch," said Conrad. "They're shadowing us."

"Why?" asked Gabe. "What's their stake in this, anyway?"

"Maybe the fellows who joined up with Sandoval are Gebhardt's men," said Conrad. "He was plenty mad at you boys when he was complaining to Gillaspy. Might be that Gebhardt has thrown in with Sandoval."

Thurston recalled the German's anger when his four sons had themselves a little fun with that fellow, Tidwell. If Gebhardt was still nursing a grudge, it would go a long way to explaining their reception at the ranch and the riders who were tailing them.

"You've got a point, Conrad. As I remember it, the boys mixed it up with Tidwell pretty good. They had to carry him over to the doc's place."

"What do you reckon them riders plan to do?" said Thad.

"I don't know."

That was true, but he figured they'd make a nuisance of themselves at the very least. At worst, they'd attack. He'd heard that the German was paying top dollar to his hands, so there might even be some gunfighters in his outfit.

Conrad rode over beside him. "Boss, if we attack Sandoval and his pards, them Gebhardt men will start shootin' at us sure as sin. Between the two, we don't stand the chance of a keg of beer at a wake."

Thurston was adding things up the same way.

"All right," he said with considerable reluctance. "We'll break it off and head back for town."

"You mean to say that you're going to give up and let Sandoval get away," said Gabe.

His middle son knew how to hurt him.

"I'm never giving up," he said. "Don't you believe it for a minute. But we've got to back off for now. We've got no choice. We'll pick up Ben on our way. When we get to Piedmont, we'll post a reward. A big one. We'll spread dodgers all over the Territory if we have to. With every mother's son looking to get that reward money, Sandoval won't live past Christmas. He'll be hunted like a rabid dog. And with a little luck, we'll get them others along with him."

It was barely light when Jake heard the rider approaching. They were all awake.

"We've got company," he warned.

"I see him," said Tidwell. "He's from the ranch. Name is Chung Li."

They were waiting for him when he rode into camp. Chung Li was small in stature and dressed in worn jeans and a plaid flannel shirt. Beneath his wide-brimmed hat were bright, alert eyes that probably didn't miss much.

"I was sent with a message," he said.

"Then light and sit," said Jake. "Coffee will be ready in a little while." He'd changed his mind and decided to risk building a small fire beneath the trees where the smoke would be filtered by the branches.

Chung Li dismounted and tied the reins of his horse to a pine tree.

"It is about the men who follow you."

His English was spoken with an accent, betraying his origins.

"Mr. Gebhardt ordered several of us to shadow them. To stay back, but to let them see us and know that we would intervene in any trouble they started."

"Then we're indebted," said Jake.

Chung Li acknowledged his gratitude.

"The plan worked," he continued. "After a time, they broke off their pursuit and turned south. I was sent to tell you of this event."

"I wonder what Thurston is going to do now?" said Decker. "He's not the kind who'll give up easy."

"He's only backed off because he lost the advantage," said Jake. "You can bet that he's not going to crawl back under his rock and forget about Miguel."

While they took the time to eat breakfast, Jake considered his own next move.

"You're plotting," said Decker. "I can tell by that look."

Jake grinned in spite of himself. "I'm afraid you caught me."

"Well? Are you going to let us in on it?"

"All right. I'm thinking about hiring out as a cowhand. Since they don't know me, I'm the one that should infiltrate Thurston's ranch and see what I can find out. I've got a strong feeling that there's more going on here than a simple robbery. There's got to be some reason why Ben lied about Miguel."

"You mean you're just going to ride up and ask for a job?" said Decker.

Jake shrugged. "Well, after all, they're a hand short. Maybe they'll hire me."

"If I'd had my druthers," said Tidwell, "that outfit would have come on up here. I wanted a crack at 'em."

Jake downed the last of his coffee. "It's likely you'll still get your chance," he said. "When that time comes, you're to follow my orders. Understand?"

Tidwell looked down at his hands. "Understood," he mumbled.

"What we need," said Decker, "is a place to hole up. Someplace that's close to town and to the Thurston ranch, as well."

Tidwell looked up. "Hey, I know a place that might do. But it ain't much, I guess. An old adobe that was abandoned a long time ago. It's close to a draw, northwest of Piedmont. I took shelter there one time when a rainstorm came up sudden-like."

"It sounds like what we need," said Jake. "Lead the way amigo."

It was a two-day ride down the mountain and out on the flat. Always, they were cautious. Besides the Apache threat, there was the chance that Thurston would change his mind and backtrack to trail them once Gebhardt's men backed off.

Come nightfall, they camped in a high-walled canyon.

The steep sides were dotted with mesquite, creosote bushes, and cholla. During heavy rains in the mountains, the run-off would fill the bottom, making a river. But now, it was dry.

Though not alone, Jake was touched by a sense of loneliness. All who shared the campfire had been drawn there by the dangerous arrogance of one man. Off in the distance, a lone coyote howled at the moon. Jake figured he knew how the creature felt.

They broke camp early and continued on through the canyon, topping out on the desert when the sun was high. It was late afternoon when Tidwell spotted the adobe shack he was looking for. When they drew near, Jake noticed that most of the roof was still intact. So were the four walls. They rode up and dismounted. Around the doorway lay broken shards of pottery. An *olla* sat beside it, empty of the water it was created to hold. A quick inspection told him there was enough water in the nearby draw to satisfy the horses' thirst. There was also a natural *tinaja* in back that was half full.

Inside the shack, signs remained that others had camped there before them. They set about brushing out the place. But even with order restored, the shack wasn't much. It would, however, provide shelter from the elements. If need be, it could serve as a fortress of sorts from their enemies.

Over their evening meal, Decker made an announcement.

"Come morning, I'm going to ride into town. Snooping around is what I'm good at. When I get to Piedmont, I intend to do a lot of it. Might find out something interesting."

Jake had misgivings. "Can you be sure that no one saw you when you were there before?" he asked.

"Reasonably. Not only did the jailbreak grab everyone's attention, but the town was in an uproar about the Apaches' attack south of there. Besides, I didn't linger long. I'll be fine."

Jake hoped he was right. At any rate, it was impossible for any of the rest of them to take Decker's place. They were all known, himself as well. Gillaspy and Walkenshaw had seen him, as the hangman, and the hostler and barkeep knew him as a rancher passing through. Besides, he had his own job to do.

"All right," he agreed. "I'm leaving in the morning too. Miguel, you stay here with Tidwell and Chung Li. Wait for word from me or Decker."

Decker looked pleased with himself. But not Tidwell. He wandered off and sat staring at the sky. Again, he would have to wait for the vengeance he wanted so badly.

That night sleep didn't come easy to Jake. They'd left the horses picketed close by and were relying on them to warn of any approaching danger. Still, a man got used to relying on himself. Besides there was the fact that a lot of things could go wrong. This was what played on his mind and kept him awake.

Chapter Six

When sleep finally came, Jake's dreams were all about Alicia and the ranch he'd built a few days' ride from Phoenix. He'd stocked it using part of the gold he'd retrieved from the Mazatzal Mountains, the gold cache that his Uncle Nate had discovered.

It was on this trek across the Sonoran Desert that he'd rescued Ryan Decker, then a greenhorn kid. On his return, he'd come across Alicia and Miguel. He'd given them his protection and ended up with a family.

When he opened his eyes it was still dark. Only the sounds of snoring disturbed the silence. In the quiet of his own mind, he considered the elements of his dreams and felt a longing to be home. He'd be there now, if only Miguel hadn't been spurred by discontent. But it was difficult, if not impossible, to keep others from their folly. He recalled how Decker had recklessly sought adventure, but Decker had matured.

Outside the window openings of their hideaway, it was starting to get light. Soon the others began to stir. Jake got up and pulled on his boots for he and Decker would soon be leaving. Though they'd be heading for different destinations, both places held potential dangers.

Chung Li, a man of many talents, set to work fixing a meal of pan bread and bacon. He opened a can of peaches and put the coffee on to boil. It wasn't long before they were eating breakfast around a fire that took off the morning chill.

When they'd finished, Decker set about getting ready to leave. While Chung Li and Miguel cleaned up, Tidwell motioned Jake to follow him outside.

"What is it?" Jake asked.

"I don't like hanging around this place doing nothing. I'd figured on some action."

"Like what?"

"Like getting one of the Thurstons in my gun sights."

The man was starting to irritate him.

"Look, it may come to that," he said. "Meanwhile, we're trying to save this boy's neck and find the real killer."

"Then you expect me to sit here on my backside and whittle and whistle while you two go off on your own?"

Jake fixed him with a stare. "That's about the size of it. But look at it this way. You're a bodyguard. You're keeping Thurston and his boys from having what they want most in the world—the life of Miguel Sandoval."

"Yeah," said Tidwell, looking like he'd just had a revelation. "When you put it that way, it don't seem so bad."

"Then wait here with Miguel and Chung Li until you

hear from one of us. Before this is over, you'll have your chance at the Thurstons."

Decker stepped outside. He'd shaved off his stubble, cleaned himself up, and was wearing fresh clothes from his saddlebag.

"Do you think I look like an up-and-coming newspaper reporter?" he asked.

"You sure pass muster with me," said Jake, "but do you think you can fool the citizens of Piedmont?"

Decker made a face. "I resent that. Until I stood up to that tyrant of an editor and got myself fired, I was, in fact, an up-and-coming reporter."

"Don't worry," said Jake. "You will be again. You can't help yourself. What you ought to do is take some of your share of that gold we toted down from the Mazatzal Mountains and start your own newspaper."

Decker gave him a lopsided grin. "I've thought about that, believe me. If I can find the right town, I think I will. That is, if we can ever get out of this mess."

"One way or another, we're going to settle things," said Jake. "You can count on it."

Decker saddled his horse, tightened the cinch, and mounted up. "Well, here goes," he said. "Take care of yourself, my friend."

With a wave to the others, he rode off in the direction of Piedmont.

Jake watched for a time as the horse and rider grew smaller with distance. Then he went over and saddled the blood bay.

Miguel followed and stood close by.

"I'm leaving those town-bought horses here with

you," said Jake. "There's too much of a chance they'd be recognized. I'm leaving the dun, as well."

"Good thinking," said Miguel. "Be careful, now. If anything happened to you, my sister would never forgive me."

"I'll do my best."

Jake stepped into leather and headed the blood bay toward the Thurston ranch. The sun had cleared the mountains and was already warming the night-cooled landscape.

He wondered if Thurston's vigilantes had gone directly to Piedmont to report to Gillaspy, or if they'd doubled back to the mountains. He was betting on the former, since Gebhardt's riders would have stuck with them if they'd doubled back. One thing Thurston wouldn't want was to be caught between enemy forces.

Jake wasn't worried about Santos' village, either. Eduardo Santos wasn't a trusting man. His people were armed and well able to defend themselves.

What Jake had to do now was turn himself into an actor. He had to make them think he was a thirty-a-month saddle bum who was looking for a job; a fellow that had no quarrel with the Thurston clan. Even though he was gold-wealthy and owned a large cattle ranch, the first part would be easy. Until a couple of years earlier, he'd actually been a ranch hand in California, making a dollar a day. But the second part, the one about having no quarrel with the cattle baron and his sons, would be harder. He doubted that he could even look Thurston in the eye without revealing the contempt he felt. That is, if it ever came to that. *Hey, you can do what you have to do,* he thought.

It was later in the day when he arrived at Thurston's ranch, the Tumbling T. He was intercepted right off by a couple of hard-faced cowhands. Both wore sidearms and had rifles in their saddle scabbards.

"What is it you want?" the bigger one demanded. If a man could have a swagger in his voice, this one did.

"I want to talk to your boss about a job."

"We don't need no help," he said. "Now, turn around and git."

"Wait a minute, Hogue," said his partner. "Conrad might be needing someone. Remember?"

The two exchanged glances. A light dawned in Hogue's eyes as he was reminded of the vacancy caused by Wade's death.

"Yeah," he agreed, "the foreman might want to see you. Stay here with Shorty."

While Jake waited, he looked around at the pole corral, the barn, and the many outbuildings. The main house itself was better than what he'd expected. It wasn't as big and impressive as Gebhardt's place, but it wasn't bad, either. A fit dwelling for a land baron.

A good distance away from the main house, a long, narrow bunkhouse bellied up against the land. If he got the job, he figured that was where he'd be hanging his hat. At least when he wasn't out on the range.

Shorty wasn't talkative. Jake let it be and just sat there, appearing disinterested. The wait was awkward, but at last Hogue reappeared.

"All right, Conrad wants to see you up at the barn. Hand over your guns."

"I kind of like to keep hold of 'em. Don't feel right without 'em."

Hogue gave him a mean look. "Do what you're told and don't get smart."

Jake reached down and unbuckled his gun belt, handing it over.

"Now, the rifle. Draw it up easy-like."

He relinquished the new Winchester that Alicia had given him to replace his old Spencer Carbine. Except for his knife, he was weaponless in the enemy camp. Every nerve was alert.

"Now, get down off that nag and follow me," Hogue ordered.

When they reached the other side of the barn, Thurston's foreman looked up. Jake recalled seeing him in Piedmont. He hoped the reverse wasn't true. But since he'd had his hat pulled low and had stood to one side, he doubted that Conrad had gotten a look at him.

The man before him appeared to be ordinary in every way. In fact, he was so nondescript that he could go unnoticed in a crowd, except for one thing—his eyes. Smoky gray in color, they were shrewd and observant. Jake guessed that not much was missed by the foreman of the Tumbling T.

"Hogue tells me you're here for a job," he said after taking Jake in with a glance.

"Yeah. I heard that Thurston was the biggest rancher in this part of Arizona."

"Where'd you work before?"

Without hesitation, he answered. "Place down south.

A few days' ride from Phoenix. Before that, California. North of Los Angeles."

"What's your moniker?"

Jake saw no reason to lie. "Lockridge. Jake Lockridge."

"All right, Lockridge, you're hired. So long as you ride for the brand and do your job like you're told, you'll stay hired. If you don't. Well, that's another matter."

"I'll do the job," Jake assured him.

"Then Hogue, here, will show you to the bunkhouse where you can stow your stuff. He tells me you're armed with a Colt .44 and a Winchester."

"Yes."

"Got plenty of ammunition?"

"Some. If I need more, I'll holler."

With that, he was dismissed. Hogue escorted him to the bunkhouse.

"All right, Lockridge, you start work in the morning," he said. "And I mean early. You're going to get some chores done around here. You'll do whatever you're told to do. Later on, if you stack up, you'll ride out to see to the cattle. If you've got any complaints, bring 'em to me or to Conrad. Stay away from the boss. He's got his own troubles and he doesn't want to be bothered with yours."

"Understood," said Jake, keeping his expression bland.

"Then grub is ready at six or thereabouts."

When Decker entered the town of Piedmont for the second time, he saw that the gallows was still standing. He shuddered involuntarily. His first stop was at the ho-

tel where he rented a room. The desk clerk gave him
the key to a front room on the second floor. When he
opened the door and took a look at it, he was pleasantly
surprised. It contained a decent bed, an armoire, a
chair, a small table with a lamp, and a cabinet with a
pitcher and bowl on top. It wasn't too bad.

Next, he went to the livery stable where he left the
gray to be curried and given a bait of oats. It was there
that he saw the hand-printed notice tacked to the wall.
Matt Thurston was offering a five-hundred-dollar reward for Miguel Sandoval, dead or alive, and another
three hundred for his accomplice. Both were huge
amounts. There was a clear description of Miguel, not
that it was needed. There was also a sketchy description
of Jake that could apply to half the men in the Territory.
It seemed that Thurston had no qualms about seizing
authority. Authority to which he had no claim. Decker
fought the urge to rip the poster down and tear it to
shreds.

The following day, he eased into his new role. Without attracting a lot of attention, he went about town and
learned what he could. It wasn't much. On the second
full day after his arrival, he headed for one of the saloons, the one called the Vulture's Nest. The hour was
early so there was plenty of room at the bar.

"What'll you have?" asked the bartender.

"Whiskey, and I'll take it over to one of the empty
tables."

"Suit yourself."

He served the drink, and Decker removed himself to
a corner table where he could watch the room without

seeming to do so. Miguel had told him about this place; he'd learned of it from Deputy Walkenshaw, who'd mentioned that this was where Gillaspy and his crowd often hung out. Vulture's Nest was an apt name, Decker thought.

He sat there toying with the whiskey glass. He drank only rarely and then very little. Frankly, he didn't much like the taste. But when you came into a saloon, you ordered a drink. His would last a long time.

An upright piano stood against one wall, its bench vacant. He wondered if it was one of those contraptions that used paper rolls with holes to make music, rather than relying on a musician. It wasn't long before he learned that it was played manually. A woman in her early twenties came downstairs and seated herself at the instrument. Her appearance was unlike that of the typical saloon girl. Instead of being attired in a gaudy low-cut gown, her frock was dark blue and high at the neck. She eschewed the bright face paint that saloon girls always wore, leaving her coloring natural. Her dark hair was pulled back into a sleek kind of bun that was held by a silver filigreed comb. All in all, she was beautiful. He looked down at the glass in his hands in order to keep from staring at her. She began by playing a piece that he recognized as Beethoven's "Für Elise," one of his grandfather's favorites. He glanced around the sparsely filled room, curious as to the patrons' reaction to this classical piece. A few were listening with pleasure. The rest were ignoring it.

Moments later, Gillaspy entered the saloon in the company of two prominent-looking men. They seated themselves at a nearby table.

"Whiskey!" shouted Gillaspy. "And play something decent on that piano, girl!"

Decker could only see her back now, as she switched to pounding out "Little Brown Jug." The incongruity was startling and he had to suppress a laugh.

Why was a young woman with her talent, and obvious gentle rearing, playing the piano in a place like the Vulture's Nest? He figured there was a story behind that. But there was no time to ponder such a thing for he found himself eavesdropping on Gillaspy's conversation.

"Thurston is going to make big trouble if that killer ain't hanged, and soon. When he rode through here on his way back, he was so mad he could've bit a railroad spike in two. He's blaming us that Sandoval got away."

"It appears to me that he's blaming you, Gillaspy," said the beefy man with heavy jowls. "I'm just the mayor. You're the sheriff. It's your job to find Sandoval."

"And don't try to get me involved in this, either," said his companion. "I may be on the town council, but I don't approve of the way that boy was railroaded. How do we know that Ben Thurston was telling the truth? Why, I've heard him lie out both sides of his mouth at the same time."

"Shut up, Grady!" ordered Gillaspy. "The walls around Piedmont have ears. You want to let Thurston get wind of what you're saying? He'll burn that fleabag hotel of yours without a minute's hesitation."

"If my hotel is burned, I will assume that Thurston gave the order, but I expect you'll be the one to strike the match."

The air was electric with tension. Decker held his breath, waiting to see what would happen next.

"Please calm down, gentlemen," pleaded the mayor. "Nobody is going to burn anything. We're just three friends sharing our concerns."

"Yeah?" said Gillaspy. "Just what is your concern, Mr. Mayor? Didn't you like the trial, either?"

"Now, I didn't say that. I only said that it happened too quickly. We should have taken some time, looked into the matter. Given the judge a chance to sober up a little. Matt Thurston doesn't own this town and we shouldn't hang a man on his say-so, nor on Ben Thurston's story, either."

Gillaspy turned red in the face and slammed his hand down on the tabletop. Both men jumped as if they'd been shot. It attracted everyone's attention for "Little Brown Jug" had come to an end and there had been relative silence in the Vulture's Nest.

"I want all of you to know that I'm the sheriff here," said Gillaspy in a loud voice. "What I say goes. I ain't about to tolerate any whispering or gossiping about the job I'm doing. I won't tolerate any bad-mouthing of my good friends, the Thurstons, either. You'd better pay attention to this warning and pass it along. If you don't, that gallows out there might well be used for other hangings besides Sandoval's."

His unveiled threat came as a shock to everyone in the saloon. Decker could scarcely believe what he was hearing.

Having said his piece, Gillaspy stormed out, leaving the batwing doors swinging wildly behind him.

Decker heard the mayor heave a sigh of relief that he was gone.

"No-account flunky," said the hotel owner under his breath. "Wouldn't be surprised if he was the one who killed Wade and stole the money. He was sure quick to side with Ben and plenty eager to get that kid hung."

"Well, there's nothing you or me can do about it," said the mayor. "Better keep your mouth shut and get along as best you can. Try not to rile Gillaspy any more. He's stirred up enough as it is."

"Why? Are you worried that Thurston will withdraw his money from your bank?"

The mayor leaned forward and spoke in a soft voice that Decker could barely hear. "I'm worried about getting shot in the back, and you should be too."

There was a scraping of chair legs as both the mayor and the hotel owner got up and left the saloon without ordering. Decker, still nursing his drink, mulled over what he'd heard. It seemed that not everyone in town was in favor of the Thurston-Gillaspy alliance. What's more, not everyone was in favor of hanging Miguel. There were a lot of doubts. This, at least, was encouraging. Perhaps he could find out more. The theory that Gillaspy was the thief and murderer was interesting. It was even plausible. But Ben Thurston had to be in on it, somehow. He was the only witness.

The pianist resumed playing. Decker was pleased to note that "Little Brown Jug" had been replaced with "Moonlight Sonata." With Gillaspy gone, no one in the Vulture's Nest was complaining.

He sat there listening to the soothing music until his

drink was gone and he could no longer pretend he had a reason for lingering without reordering. When he left the saloon, strains of something from Bach followed him outside. He found himself humming all the way to his hotel room.

Chapter Seven

Jake was rousted out of his bunk before dawn. The light of a single candle threw shadows across the yellowed, newspaper-covered walls.

"Come on, get a move on, you saddle bums," said Hogue. "We ain't got all morning to waste."

Jake wasn't sure where in the pecking order Hogue stood, but he appeared to take pleasure in giving orders in the foreman's absence.

Grumbling at the rude awakening, the men crawled out of their beds and got dressed. Jake pulled on his boots and ran his hand across the lengthening stubble on his chin, a stubble he kept to serve as a disguise should it be needed.

Breakfast consisted of fried potatoes, boiled beef, and biscuits, accompanied by gallons of coffee. He had to admit that the cook didn't stint. As soon as the meal was over, Hogue came up to him.

"Your job is to build a new pole corral over yonder. Shorty will show you where."

Jake spent the morning laboring on the corral. Shorty threw in a word of advice now and again, and even added some elbow grease. It was late afternoon when Hogue rode up to see how much he'd got done. He looked it over and went on without a word.

"You've done good," said Shorty. "Otherwise, he'd of chewed you out."

"He the boss?"

"Thinks he is. He's bucking for Conrad's job. Everybody knows it but Conrad."

"I'm surprised one of the sons hasn't taken the job. One of the big ones or maybe the scrawny one."

Shorty chuckled. "That scrawny fellow ain't no son. The little churn-head is the boss's nephew. Though he's older than he looks. He's twenty-two. As old as Thad. His name is Roger Byrd but everyone calls him Birdie."

Jake knew that "churn-head" was what some cowhands called a dumb horse. It appeared that Shorty didn't have a high opinion of the nephew.

"He sure enough don't look like his cousins," Jake said as he put the last crossbar in place.

"No reason he should. His ma was the boss's sister. She died when he was still a little kid. Don't know who his pa was. Don't guess that boy will ever amount to anything."

From what little Jake had seen, Birdie wasn't being given much of a chance. Only the menial chores had been assigned to him.

"Well," said Shorty, "best we get these tools put up before Hogue comes sashaying past us again."

Jake took his time gathering them up, not much caring what Hogue thought. There was a lot of swagger in the man, but Jake sensed an undercurrent of unease, as well. It might be that Hogue was hiding something. For sure, he'd bear watching.

That night they ate supper around a big campfire. Again, the cook had outdone himself. Jake caught sight of Birdie sitting off by himself. Figuring it would be a good chance to get acquainted, he picked up his plate and walked over to him.

"Mind if I join you?" he asked.

Birdie looked up, surprised.

"If you've got a mind to, go ahead."

Jake found a spot close by and eased himself to the ground. It had been a long day and he was tired and hungry. He was spooning beans into his mouth when he noticed the quiet. He looked up to see the others staring at him.

"Well, well," said the one he recognized as Ben. "Two of a kind. Birds of a feather, as they say."

The others laughed and Birdie lowered his eyes.

"Something wrong?" asked Jake as he eyed Ben.

"Nope. You two belong together, but don't try sitting with the rest of us. You just ain't up to snuff."

It appeared that Ben was spoiling for a fight.

"Reckon that depends on what you mean by 'snuff,'" said Jake. "But I'm happy with the company I keep. Don't need no other."

"Remember that," said Ben. "You ain't gettin' no other."

With the prospect of a fight ended, the others went back to eating. Keeping his head lowered and his attention on his plate, Birdie did the same.

Shorty had told Jake that Ben and his brothers slept in the big house. So did Birdie. Jake wondered what kind of arrangements they'd made since they'd decided that Birdie wasn't good enough to eat with. One thing was for sure, all wasn't flowers and sunshine in the Thurston family. If Ben couldn't abide his cousin, maybe he hadn't been able to abide his brother Wade. And, after all, Ben was the one who'd lied under oath.

The following morning, Jake was ordered to clean out the barn. It was a comedown from corral building. Still, it was honest work and he set about doing it. He wasn't at it long before Birdie arrived to curry the horses. This was another chance to get acquainted.

When Jake greeted him, he merely nodded and set to work. It was several minutes before he spoke.

"Lockridge, do you know why I'm not over there shoveling horse droppings instead of curry combing this nag?"

Jake straightened up and leaned on his shovel. "I expect it's because Conrad ordered me to do it."

"Yeah. You're the stranger, the newcomer. They don't trust you and they're keeping a close watch. You'll be given the dirtiest jobs there is. And it didn't help your cause any when you came over and sat beside me last night. They like to keep me in my place. I'm their court jester, so to speak."

Jake had pretty much figured that out. Having some-one like Birdie to pick on made the Thurstons feel big-ger and stronger.

"What's even worse," he went on, "is Wade's death. They're all stirred up and hunting for a man they claim is the killer. He had an accomplice when he broke jail and nobody's too clear on what the fellow looked like. He posed as a hangman, but Gillaspy never paid much attention to him. Neither did the deputy who was on duty when the jailbreak happened."

"So every stranger is suspect."

"That's about the size of it."

"Well, I always did have bad timing. Do you think Hogue or Conrad suspects me?"

Birdie shrugged. "Look at it from their point of view. It's possible. Anyway, they'll be keeping an eye on you until you prove yourself."

"What will happen then?"

He grimaced. "Then I expect I'll be back to shovel-ing horse manure."

His voice was filled with bitterness. Jake tried to imagine what it must be like being a part of the family, yet not a part. Ostracized by the others and used as the brunt of jokes and sarcasm. Still, Birdie was far from being a child.

"Look, the way things are, why don't you saddle your horse and leave?" Jake asked. "You can get a job somewhere else. A lot better one than what you've got."

Birdie's laugh was humorless. "Don't you think I've tried? Uncle Matt brings me back. You see, I play an important part in this family. Because of me, he can think of himself as charitable, a good brother to his dead sister, who he really didn't care for. On top of that, I make his sons look top-of-the-heap by comparison."

It was a bleak picture. Birdie wasn't awful much better off than the former plantation slaves. The setting was different was all.

"Have you tried more than once to get away?"

"Oh yes," he said, "a couple of times before I was fifteen. Uncle Matt caught me and learned me better with a horse whip."

Jake felt sorry for him. He deserved better. Every human being deserved better.

"Maybe, someday, you'll get another chance, Birdie," he said, hoping it sounded encouraging.

He'd scarcely finished speaking when Hogue appeared in the doorway. "Is this a ladies' social club, or do you two intend to get some work done?"

Birdie's pale face flushed with color and he went to currying with a vengeance.

"I'm doing my job," said Jake. "No law against talking."

"Well, around here it's smart to keep your mouth shut."

While Jake and Birdie worked, Hogue watched from the doorway. He stood there a long time before turning and walking away.

When he was out of earshot, Birdie muttered an oath under his breath. "I hate that man. I truly do."

Jake glanced over at him.

"I don't usually offer advice, amigo. But it would be best to keep that sentiment to yourself. I'm thinking that Hogue can be a very dangerous enemy."

"That's like telling me the sky is blue. I don't know why my uncle keeps him around, anyway. There's nothing he does that anybody here couldn't do a lot better."

"You'll get no argument from me."

They worked in silence for a time. Then Birdie spoke up.

"I hope they keep you on, Lockridge. You're the only one that's treated me right. But be careful. None of 'em would think twice about shooting you, or even lynching you, for that matter."

"By *them* I take it you mean your uncle and your cousins."

"Hogue too. Maybe even Conrad. He don't show it, but I think he's worried."

"I expect he's thinking Hogue might take his job."

"He don't let on like he knows it, but he's not dumb. The way Hogue steps in and acts like he's got authority was surely reported."

"Looks like Conrad would set Hogue straight, or else complain to your uncle about him."

Birdie spat in disgust.

"My uncle likes situations that pit one man against another. He thinks it keeps people on their toes. As for Conrad setting Hogue straight, he'd have to shoot him. Hogue's twice his size."

The situation was clear now, and Jake felt like he'd made a friend on the Tumbling T. This was something he hadn't expected.

At mealtime they ate in the mess. Birdie took his usual place at the end, away from the others. Jake took his plate and sat down next to Shorty.

"Come on up here, Birdie," he said. "There's plenty of room."

Birdie's face flushed and he looked uncertain about what to do.

"He ain't movin'," said Ben. "He's staying right where he is."

Jake stood up and stared Ben in the eye. "Are you the social secretary who puts out the place cards?"

There was a snicker from one of the men.

"Why, you no good . . . !" Ben jumped to his feet. His hand went for his gun but Jake's .44 had already cleared leather. As Ben stood staring down the barrel, sweat slicked his face.

The others looked frozen in place. Matt Thurston had arrived in time to see the confrontation from the doorway.

"You're a mite slow, Ben," he said. "Your hot head will get you a bullet between the eyes one of these days."

He turned to Jake.

"You've got a fast draw there, mister. I admire a man who can clear leather like that. I owe you for not killing that hothead boy of mine, but if you had I'd have plugged you a second later."

"He started it," said Ben.

"I reckon he did. Birdie can sit wherever he pleases and it ain't none of your business, Ben. You understand?"

"I understand," said Ben, his rage unconcealed.

He'd been beaten to the draw and he'd shown fear in front of the men, as well as his brothers and cousin. On top of that, he'd been publicly humiliated by his father. Birdie had won a victory at his expense and the one responsible was Jake Lockridge. Jake knew he'd made a dangerous enemy.

That night in his bunk he slept lightly with his pistol under the blanket. As he was drifting off to sleep, he wondered how Decker was making out in Piedmont. His friend worried him, riding in there alone. Still, Decker was resourceful and a good observer. He had a way of getting strangers to open up to him, and whatever he accomplished would be more than what Jake had managed to do.

About all he'd learned during his time at the ranch was the fact there were divisions. Not only in the family, but in the rivalry between Conrad and Hogue. If he were in Conrad's place, he wouldn't be turning his back on Hogue. But then, he had troubles of his own. He wasn't about to turn his back on Ben Thurston.

When they were rousted from their beds the next morning, it was by none other than Matt Thurston himself.

"Get a move on," he ordered. "We're forming ourselves a posse. We're going after that killer again. I know he's still around here somewhere, him and that partner of his."

Jake was dismayed. If they headed north and happened on to that adobe, the three men inside wouldn't stand a chance. What's more, there was little he could do to help them.

He dressed quickly and strapped on his .44. Thurston allowed them time for breakfast, but very little. When Jake got to the corral, he whistled for the blood bay. It came trotting over and nuzzled his hand.

"We're taking a ride today, my friend. But we may not like what happens."

He put the rigging on and mounted up. No sooner was he in the saddle than Hogue started yelling.

"Hurry up! Get a move on! The boss is ready to pull out."

Jake noticed that Hogue was topped by a new hat. One that didn't come cheap. Not only that, he was wearing a fresh store-bought shirt and sporting a new revolver with pearl inlaid grips. If it was attention that Hogue wanted, he was getting it. He'd skipped breakfast with the men and they, too, were seeing him for the first time that day. One would have to say that Hogue was doing right well on his thirty-a-month wages. Jake wondered if any of the others were thinking the same thing.

"Hey, Hogue!" yelled Ben, a smirk on his face. "Did you get yourself all fancied up to visit a lady?"

It was an obvious struggle, but Hogue managed to keep his mouth shut. Only one of the Thurstons would dare to rib him about his attire. The more Jake knew of the man, the less he liked him. On that point, he and Birdie agreed.

Matt Thurston rode at the head of the group. Always mindful of the impression he made on others, he was mounted on a magnificent black gelding with a silver-studded saddle. But no matter how impressive he looked, he was outside the law, and he was leading what amounted to a band of vigilantes.

To Jake's relief, they headed east. When they'd left the ranch far behind, Thurston reined up.

"All right," he said, facing them, "we're going to ride

to that Mexican village over toward the mountains. They run us off once when we went to look for that killer. They won't this time. They've got a dozen men is all, and we'll take 'em by surprise."

"But, Pa, I counted more'n that," said Thad. "There's at least twice as many and they'll be watching out for us."

Thurston fixed him with a stare. "You talk out of turn again and I'll knock you out of that saddle."

But it was too late. The others were exchanging warning looks. Ben tried to salvage the situation.

"Little brother, you can't count past ten with your gloves off."

This brought a guarded chuckle from a few. But they knew the score. They also knew that Thurston had tracked the so-called killer past the village on to the mountains. What he was planning was purely an act of vindictiveness.

"What we'll do is split up," said Thurston. "We'll hit 'em from two sides. Shoot 'em right down in that draw, if that's where they're holed up."

"That'll teach 'em," said Ben. A malicious look betrayed his total lack of human compassion.

Jake felt sick inside. Whatever happened, a lot of innocents would likely be killed. He figured it was his fault, too, for riding in there in the first place and involving those people in his troubles.

When they stopped to give the horses a breather, Birdie got him off to one side.

"You want to know why my uncle is so stirred up about attacking that village?" he said, his voice low so that the others couldn't hear.

"He suspects that Sandoval is hiding there, I guess."

"No. That's just an excuse. He's mad because they stood up to him when he went looking before. A bunch of 'em drew down on him and sent us packing. That's not something the old man is apt to forget."

"There seems to be some disagreement as to their strength."

"Thad's right. The old man's lying. He doesn't want to spook the rest of 'em."

Ben noticed them in conversation and glared. "Trouble," Jake said under his breath. But before Ben could act, Thurston gave the order to ride.

Jake was relieved that they were bypassing Piedmont. There was always the risk that Gillaspy would recognize him.

As the miles passed, he racked his brain to come up with a way to spare the village, or at least to warn them. It turned out that the next time they stopped, Birdie beat him to it.

"Uncle Matt," he said, "there's been talk that since the Apache attack, General Crook and his men are scouting this area. When he finds out what we've done to those people, he's sure to come after us."

Thurston scowled at his nephew. "Now where in blazes did you hear that?"

"Remember? We heard it when we were in town. General Crook wouldn't tolerate us shooting a bunch of women and kids."

"That little churn-head don't know nothin'," said Ben. "Don't pay him no mind."

Birdie ignored Ben and stood his ground. There was

some grumbling among the others who were well aware of Crook's reputation. Thurston made it clear that he didn't like what he was hearing. It was one thing to kill a bunch of people when you could get away with it, but when there was sure to be repercussions, it was a different matter. He spat a wad of chewing tobacco that made a wide arc on its way to the ground.

"I wish the meddling government would stay out of my business and out of Arizona. I surely do."

Whether or not General Crook was still in the area, Thurston was plenty worried. Birdie had succeeded in getting through to him. Attack that village and there would be consequences, and not just from the villagers. While Thurston could take over a small town in the desert, he wasn't any match for the United States Army.

"What are you going to do now, Pa?" said Ben. "You ain't planning on turning back, are you?"

His father glared at him.

"Not by a long shot. But we're going to ride over to that highfalutin German's ranch. It's time he was taught a lesson or two. It'd serve him right if we was to burn that fancy place of his and tear up what won't burn. If he hadn't butted in to what wasn't none of his business, I'd have had that killer hanged by now."

Jake recalled the beauty of Gebhardt's home. It was filled with nice things that hadn't been cheap or easy to bring in. This wasn't as bad as murdering a whole village of people, but it wasn't good. It was plain that Thurston liked to kill and destroy what others had built. He was a bully by nature; he was a killer by choice.

Jake's only purpose had been to save Miguel's life.

But the situation had grown larger and more complicated. A lot of lives were at stake, as well as property. Thurston had overstepped the boundaries of the law and was, himself, an outlaw. But unless Jake could think of something to stop him, others would die and a lovely hacienda would soon go up in flames.

Chapter Eight

Decker allowed himself the luxury of sleeping late. Then, after sprucing himself up, he ventured out of his room in search of a meal. A leisurely breakfast in the hotel dining room added no new information to his collection. Leaving the dining room, he walked down the street to the mercantile. *I believe it's time to buy a new shirt,* he thought. Inside, the place smelled of licorice and leather, fresh ground coffee and cloves, as well as a variety of other scents that blended in subtly. He rummaged through a stack of shirts on a shelf and after making a selection, he engaged the proprietor in conversation. When he casually broached the subject of Miguel's trial, the man looked apprehensive.

"It's over and done with," he said abruptly. "We don't talk of such things to strangers."

When Decker apologized and started to leave, the man's relief was obvious. He was clearly frightened.

Decker decided to explore the town on foot and took pains to remain inconspicuous. Sheriff Gillaspy, on the other hand, took another approach. Like the politician he was, he made sure that everyone noticed him. Decker watched as the short, squat sheriff made his way down the street, back-slapping and glad-handing like election day was the following week. A few acted flattered by his attention. Others shied away.

Since his arrival, Decker had seen nothing of Deputy Walkenshaw. Strange, he thought. A public official dropping out of sight. Later, a discreet inquiry at the Whiskey Barrel Saloon explained the reason why.

"Gillaspy went and fired old Russ," said the barkeep. "He was a good man too. Honest as the day is long. But he got the sheriff in trouble with the Thurstons when he let that kid escape."

"They don't think he did it on purpose do they?"

The barkeep shrugged. "It's no matter. It happened on his watch so he's out of a job."

"I guess he's packed up and left Piedmont, then."

"Nope. At least not yet. He's got a place out on the edge of town, out past the church. It's the house with all the desert marigolds planted in front. His daughter's doing, I expect."

"Appreciate the information."

"If you see him, tell him Schmidt sends his regards. Tell him he's got a free drink on the house any time he wants it."

"I'll do that."

Decker left the saloon, climbed on his horse, and

went to pay Russ Walkenshaw a visit. It was easy to spot the house with the marigolds.

"My father's not receiving visitors," said the grim-faced young woman who answered his knock. "He no longer works for the sheriff."

He figured he was talking to Walkenshaw's daughter, the one who was responsible for planting the flowers.

"I realize that he was fired," he said. "I'd simply like to have a word with him on a matter of mutual interest."

"Who is it, Maybelle?" called a man's voice from the back of the house.

"Father, there's a gentleman here who wants to talk to you."

"Then tell him to come in, girl. Don't leave him standing outside."

Decker stepped into the parlor. It was neat and free of dust despite the frequent winds, which blew particles of dirt and sand through the tiniest cracks. Miss Walkenshaw was clearly a dedicated housekeeper.

"What can I do for you?" asked Walkenshaw, drying his hands on his pants legs as he entered the room.

"I've heard about the conspiracy to execute a fellow named Sandoval. It's said that Matt Thurston and your Sheriff Gillaspy railroaded him through a mockery of a trial. They were about to hang him for a crime he didn't commit."

The woman looked shocked. "You mustn't say things like that in Piedmont. You could get killed. You could get us all killed."

"I understand that, ma'am. But you see my name is

Decker, and I'm a reporter who's trying to get at the truth."

Walkenshaw grimaced. "The truth won't always set you free, my friend. Sometimes it'll get you a permanent resting place six feet under."

"What I'm wondering," said Decker, "is who will be next. It seems to me that Thurston's word alone is enough to put a rope around anyone's neck who crosses him."

"And that's why it's dangerous for you to be here asking questions," said Maybelle. "Not only for you, but for my father, as well. Did you know that Thurston ordered Gillaspy and a couple of his thugs to take Papa out and beat him? That was for being on duty when Miguel Sandoval escaped. Gillaspy—the pig—would have done it, too, but he knew the townspeople wouldn't stand for it. We're walking on eggshells, Mr. Decker."

He could see the fear in her large hazel eyes. In Walkenshaw's, he read only disillusionment and disgust.

"This used to be a pretty good town," said the ex-deputy. "That is, until the Thurston outfit moved in and took over. The old man stuffed the ballot boxes for Gillaspy, and now he plays him like a puppet. If you want to know something, just ask. I'll give you an answer if I can."

"After the robbery, did you notice any strangers around town, especially ones that were spending a conspicuous amount of money?"

Walkenshaw scratched his chin. "I see where you're headed. No, the only stranger was the one who broke the kid out of jail. And then, of course, yourself."

"You saw me? I got here after the jailbreak and was only in town long enough to discover what was going on."

"Don't worry. I doubt if Gillaspy was paying any attention. He was busy kowtowing to Thurston. Then, too, there was the panic over that Indian attack."

He hoped Walkenshaw was right about Gillaspy.

"There's something else," said Decker. "Do the Thurston brothers get along with one another?"

Walkenshaw looked thoughtful. "They present a united front here in town, but I've heard there's a lot of jockeying for the old man's favor. I expect their pa likes it that way. It helps to keep them in line."

"Do you think it's possible that one of Wade's brothers could have killed him? Maybe in a fit of anger?"

Walkenshaw shrugged.

"All right, then suppose there was rivalry over a girl. Jealousy is a powerful feeling. It might be that robbery wasn't the motive, but rather the cover-up."

Walkenshaw gave him a curious look. "Maybe you've got something there, Decker. I guess it could have been one of Wade's brothers that killed him and stole the money. Might have hidden it and then blamed everything on the first fellow he came across."

"I understand it was Ben who testified that he'd seen Sandoval do the killing."

"Yep. That's who it was. I heard him myself."

"I know for a fact he was lying. That makes Ben a prime suspect in Wade's murder."

Maybelle turned on her heel and walked out of the room. Clearly she was upset by the conversation her father was having. A look of pain crossed Walkenshaw's face.

"The question is, what can you or I, or anyone else, do about it?" he said.

"Maybe there's something. I've been thinking. It's too bad Piedmont doesn't have a newspaper. A few well-phrased questions might get folks to wanting some answers."

Walkenshaw shook his head. "It won't work. A fellow from back East tried to start a paper here about a year ago. He lasted for exactly one issue before Gillaspy ran him out of town."

"Didn't anybody stand up for that editor?"

"Nobody was fool enough to try. After they beat him up and broke his press, he hightailed it for Phoenix. Least that's where I heard he went."

Decker felt a deep sense of outrage. He wondered why this hadn't been reported in other newspapers. For his own editor, it would have been front-page news. Maybe that fellow hadn't made it to Phoenix or to anywhere else. Maybe he'd been murdered.

"I appreciate your forthrightness," he said. "And by the way, I heard how you helped Sandoval to escape. Thanks. He's a good man."

Walkenshaw gave a start. The only ones who knew about his assistance were the condemned man and the so-called hangman. He'd just been made aware that Decker had spoken to one or both of them.

"I'm glad to know they're all right," he said. "But you be careful. If they catch you, there's nothing I can do. Fact is, I'm planning on taking my daughter and leaving here just as soon as I can. Won't nobody in town hire me. They're all scared of what Gillaspy would do to them."

"I'm sorry. You've got a nice place here."

When Decker left the house, he glanced around to see if he'd been followed. There was no sign of anyone. It seemed to him that what Piedmont needed was a good stirring up. Since he was a reporter, he figured he could get the job done.

He always carried paper, pen, and ink in his saddle-bags so there would be no need to attract attention by buying any locally. Back in his hotel room, he shut the door and propped a chair beneath the knob for extra security. There were locks, but then anyone could pick up a key at the desk.

Next, he drew the curtain, lit the lamp, and began the first edition of the *Piedmont Sentinel*. He had no office, no press, no newsprint, no staff, no distributors. Still, the written word was powerful. Even a scrap of paper nailed to a wall would draw the curious to read and to question. Maybe a lot of eyes would see his editorial before it was ripped away by those it condemned.

He began by detailing the lack of investigation into Wade Thurston's killing. Next, he described the hurried, mock trial that had been presided over by a drunken judge. He suggested that the jurors had been intimidated, if not outright bribed. He included a description of the prisoner's beating by the sheriff and one of his deputies. Finally, he planted more doubt. Where was the stolen money? Was Ben Thurston's testimony credible? Why the rush to judgment? He concluded with a question. "Are you living in a democracy, or are you living under the tyranny of a vindictive cattle baron and his flunky with a tin star?"

Strong words. Words that just might have the power to heat the pot of apathy to a full boil of resistance. Words that could get their author shot in the back.

In a careful hand, he made two copies. Then he waited. While it was still dark, he slipped downstairs and out the back way. He had with him a small hammer and a handful of nails that were left over from the times he'd put up advertisements for his former boss. The main street was deserted. Even the saloons were closed and silent. The first copy, he nailed to the door of the general merchandise store. Then, keeping to the darkest places, he made his way down to the livery barn. After ripping off Thurston's reward poster and tearing it in half, he affixed the second copy of his *Sentinel*. Let them wonder who wrote it. He trusted the Walkenshaws to keep his secret.

His task completed, he went back to his hotel room and packed. Once it was light outside, he'd no longer be safe. There was the ink, pen, and paper that would incriminate him. He dared not throw them away, nor could he pack them with his things. If he were detained, they'd be searched. He had to hide them someplace where they wouldn't be found. He looked around the room. There was only one possibility. He took them, rolled up the paper and thrust them into a large enamel chamber pot with a lid. Then he pushed it back inside the cabinet that was provided to conceal such a personal necessity. It wasn't a foolproof hiding place, but it was the best he could do.

Shortly after dawn the town started waking up. He went to the curtained window and watched, taking care to keep out of sight. It wasn't long before he observed the first readers of the *Piedmont Sentinel*. In front of the general merchandise store, a few curious citizens quickly turned into a small gathering. Gillaspy, on his way to the café for morning coffee, crossed the street to see what all the hubbub was about.

Decker quietly eased the window open a notch in order to hear what was being said.

"What the dickens is going on here?" the sheriff demanded to know.

"There on the door." Someone pointed to the editorial.

The crowd parted, making way for Gillaspy to pass among them.

"Who put this here?" he yelled when he'd finished reading.

No one volunteered.

"It was here when I arrived this morning," said the storekeeper.

"Then why didn't you yank it down?"

"Didn't know what it was. Had to read it first. Then other folks came along."

In one swift motion, Gillaspy reached up and ripped it off the door. "I'm taking this for evidence," he said.

"Evidence of what?" came a question from the crowd.

This gave the sheriff pause. "Treason," he bellowed at last. "I'm going to find the criminal who wrote this and jail him for treason. Anybody who helps him is going to be arrested for treason too."

He was storming off toward the café when he noticed

another crowd had gathered down the street at the livery barn. The café was forgotten. Gillaspy headed for the barn at a trot. He was livid when he tore down the second copy. His shouted threats were clearly audible.

Decker found himself enjoying the scene. Gillaspy was riled. No longer the smiling glad-hander, he was showing his true colors. A lot of citizens had read the *Sentinel* and they were talking among themselves. It was an unsettling situation for the sheriff, causing him obvious concern. But Decker had no doubt about the danger to his own life. Those with a stranglehold on the town would soon be on another manhunt.

He was already down in the lobby, dressed in his oldest range clothes, when Gillaspy strode in with two new deputies. They looked more like outlaws than lawmen. He'd brought Grady, the hotel owner, along too. The entourage swept by Decker as if he were invisible.

"We're searching the place," Gillaspy announced to the desk clerk. "Give me the keys."

The frightened clerk looked questioningly at his employer.

"This isn't necessary," blustered Grady, "and it's violating the privacy of my guests."

Gillaspy ignored his protests and grabbed the desk clerk by his shirtfront. "I told you to give me the keys, and I ain't telling you again."

With a trembling hand, the clerk complied. The sheriff grabbed them and took the stairs two at a time, leaving the deputies and Grady to straggle along behind.

Decker judged it was time for him to make his exit. He'd left nothing in his room but those few hidden tools of his trade. He was ready to make a run for it. His horse had been grain fed and was waiting for him at the livery stable. His saddle was there and his saddlebags were slung over his shoulder. The way he had it figured, it was only a matter of time before Gillaspy found his stash. The first issue of the *Piedmont Sentinel* would also be the last.

"Good morning," he greeted the hostler. "I think I'll go for a little ride."

The hostler scratched his beard and yawned.

"Might be Apaches around," he said, "that is, if you've a mind to leave town. I hear they're plenty mad."

"No doubt. In their place, I'd be mad, too, after that massacre."

"Well, it wasn't right what was done to 'em," he allowed, "but if they catch you out there all by your lonesome, Lord help you."

Decker was thinking the same thing, only his prime concern at the moment wasn't the Apaches, but those in town who would kill to silence his voice.

With deft movements, he saddled his horse and led it outside. A quick glance told him that Gillaspy and the others hadn't finished at the hotel. The search would, no doubt, be thorough. He mounted up and rode out of town.

Nothing had been gained by coming here, he told himself. At least not much. Of course, he now suspected that one of the Thurston outfit had done the killing. His vote went to Ben. With luck, his editorial would cause others to ask questions, if only among themselves. He'd also forced Gillaspy to let down his politician's facade and show his ruthlessness and lack of respect for the law and the people. If anyone had doubts before, they had none now. In an instant he'd changed from a grinning, backslapping vote-seeker to a cold-blooded criminal. One whose mind was just a bubble off plumb.

Heading into the desert, Decker ignored the rumbling of his stomach. He wondered how much time he had before Gillaspy was on his trail. Of course, there was a chance the sheriff wouldn't find the evidence. But that wasn't something to count on. How odd, he thought, that the key to his destiny lay hidden in a scarred old chamber pot. He found himself grinning in spite of the danger. What would his grandfather, the austere Judge Kemp of Prescott, think about that?

Now that Piedmont was well behind him, he wasn't sure where to go. He dared not risk leading Gillaspy and his deputies to the adobe hideout. Neither could he go to Jake. He recalled a piece of advice his grandfather had given him years earlier.

"When you don't know what to do, Ryan, my boy, simply watch and wait, and always trust your instincts."

Of course, his grandfather had the instincts of a gambler. They were better, in fact, than those of some gamblers. For sure, the old man hadn't made many mistakes. But did he possess a gambler's instinct, himself? He wasn't sure. If any of them did, it was likely to be Jake.

Time passed with no sign of pursuit. Thankfully, there was no sign of Apaches, either. The sun was overhead now, sucking the moisture from his pores. He decided to stop for a spell and rest under the shade of a paloverde. Here he took a few sips from his canteen and looked into the distance.

It seemed like an eternity since he'd posted those editorials after staying up most of the night. With the immediate danger gone, weariness overtook him. Soon he slept. When he opened his eyes, it was late afternoon. He scolded himself for his carelessness, though the sleep had been much needed. Standing and stretching muscles that were long unused, he looked over his back trail. To his surprise, there was a single rider in the distance. Taking his rifle from its scabbard, he waited. Whoever it was, he was coming from the direction of Piedmont and he was in an awful big hurry.

When the rider drew close, he saw, to his surprise, that it was a woman. She was forking the horse like a man and was burning up the trail. He looked beyond, thinking she might be pursued. She was alone.

"What's the hurry?" he asked when she reined to a stop a dozen yards away.

"If you're Decker, I'm looking for you."

She swung down from the saddle and removed her hat. Not even the dust could obscure the beauty of her face. She was wearing a buckskin riding skirt and was armed with a Smith and Wesson pistol. He recognized her as the pianist from the Vulture's Nest. The one who'd been advertised as Emily Montclaire.

"Why are you looking for me?" he asked. "And how did you know where to find me?"

"It's simple. I followed your trail. Sheriff Gillaspy is fit to be tied. He's going to hang my best friend's father as a warning to the townspeople. The hanging is due to take place the day after tomorrow. No trial. No nothing.

He'd have done it right away, but he wants the word to get around."

"What did he do?"

"He made a couple of mistakes. He let Sandoval escape and he talked to you."

"Walkenshaw?"

"Yes."

Decker felt sick to his stomach. She was right. It was his fault. Someone must have seen him talking to Walkenshaw, after all.

"It was those editorials," she said. "They've gotten everyone stirred up. Gillaspy is scared. You can tell by looking at him. He claims that Mr. Walkenshaw wrote them, even though that's not the way he writes. Maybelle told me that you wrote them. But don't worry. She won't say anything to Gillaspy because it wouldn't do any good. He'd go ahead and kill her father anyway for conspiring with you."

Decker uttered a curse under his breath, not much caring if Emily Montclaire heard.

"Gillaspy has overstepped the boundaries," he said. "He's nothing but an outlaw. I guess they didn't find my paper and ink."

"No, not that I heard. Did you hide it well?"

"Not really. But it was the best I could do. I guess Gillaspy must not have done a thorough search of the hotel."

"My uncle, Tom Grady, owns the establishment. He was forced to accompany the sheriff when he ransacked those rooms. He despises Gillaspy and would have impeded him as much as possible."

Decker hated to appear helpless in front of such a pretty young woman.

"Miss Montclaire, I'm not sure what I can do."

She fixed him with a look of desperation.

"Well, you've got to do something and you've got to hurry. Mr. Walkenshaw doesn't have a lot of time."

Decker stepped into the saddle and looked down at her.

"You were brave riding out here all alone," he said. "Couldn't you have sent someone else?"

"There was no one. My uncle is being closely watched and so are the others. Gillaspy even threatens to send to the Thurston ranch for reinforcements. I was the only one who was able to slip out of town."

He was glad that she'd gotten word to him, but he had no idea how he was going to save Walkenshaw from the gallows. It was then that the words of his grandfather came back to him again. *Trust your instincts, my boy.*

"I'm not going back with you," he said suddenly. "I've got a plan."

"You're going to run off," she accused. "After you started this, you're going to ride away and let an innocent man hang?"

Decker felt his face flush.

"Look, I can't stand up to that bunch all by myself. I'm going for help. Maybe you'd better go with me. It's dangerous for you to be out here alone."

"I've got to go back. Maybelle is anxious for word. Besides, the renegade Apaches have retreated to their stronghold."

He hoped so, for everyone's sake.

"Please, promise you'll bring help," she begged.

"I promise. Now, time is wasting."

As he rode off, he could feel her watching him. She was skeptical and he didn't blame her. Walkenshaw's only hope was for him to reach the hideout where Miguel and the others waited. That was half of his plan. The other half was in the making.

But one thing was for sure. Now, everyone in Piedmont knew that Gillaspy was a killer wearing a star.

Chapter Nine

Thurston wasn't keeping secret the fact that burning Gebhardt's hacienda would give him a lot of satisfaction. The way Jake saw it, this was all about salving Thurston's injured pride. There was the aborted raid on the village, its previous rebuff, and then Gebhardt's unwelcome intervention. But Gebhardt sized up be tough and smart. He'd be on the alert.

Birdie, alone, appeared to disapprove of what his uncle had in mind. Jake admired his spunk and his cunning in saving the village from attack. That he'd been successful was surprising, seeing as how he was the brunt of their jokes and the one assigned to the dirty work that no one else wanted to do. In Jake's opinion the young cousin was, by far, the best of the lot.

Unfortunately the threat of General Crook wouldn't serve a second time to save the Gebhardt place. They were farther north, now, and Thurston was hot for revenge. Besides, Birdie had interfered about as much as would be tolerated. Jake figured it was his turn. When Thurston had them pull up to give the horses a blow, Jake scowled and made a point of glancing over his back trail.

"You expecting somebody?" said Ben, making the question a challenge.

He shrugged. "Maybe," he said.

Thurston overheard and looked across at him. "Do you think somebody is following us, Lockridge?"

"Could be. I caught a glimpse of something a while back. Thought it might be riders raising a little dust. No sign of 'em now, though."

"Now, who'd be following us?" said Gabe.

"Apaches might," said Thad. "Lockridge, did you see any Apaches?"

Jake shook his head. "You don't see Apaches until they want you to."

"Then who?" demanded Thurston.

Jake hoped he'd be able to pull this off as well as Birdie had.

"I've heard a lot of talk about this Gebhardt fellow, about how he has powerful friends. It's said that he's related to that German general they write so much about. Sigel, I think his name is. The one who fought with Lyon at Wilson's Creek. No doubt Gebhardt's got allies in Washington, but I hear he has them in Arizona too. It might be that they heard you were riding this way."

"I don't see how," said Ben.

"You scared?" Thurston taunted.

"More like prudent. Even if we could get away with

what you're planning, we'd be hounded. Burn down his place and Gebhardt and his allies won't rest until you're dead."

"Oh, yeah?" said Ben. "What if the high-and-mighty Gebhardt gets a bullet in the head?"

"In that case, I expect his friends would be even more anxious to find you."

He watched their expressions. He'd tried to put the fear in them. Let them know there would be consequences.

Thad looked scared. Ben seemed unconvinced. The others were waiting to hear what the old man would say. Thurston appeared torn.

"Pa," said Thad, "I think maybe Lockridge is right. Maybe we ought to turn around and go back home."

"Shut up!" yelled Thurston. "I'm the one that does the thinking around here."

The tension grew heavy as he wrestled with a decision. It was hard for such a man to back down twice. Still, he was aware that Gebhardt was rich and powerful. Unlike the cowed townspeople, when the German was pushed, he was going to push back. Hard. He looked up and singled out Jake.

"Are you sure you saw somebody following us, Lockridge, or are you just a yellow belly who jumps at every shadow?"

He'd made Jake a target for venting his anger and frustration. The situation was dangerous. Everyone knew it. All eyes were watching him. The next few minutes would determine whether Jake would live or die. The .44 was heavy on his hip, but he wouldn't stand a chance against them all. A picture of Alicia formed in his mind, her beautiful eyes and long dark hair. He groped for words that would deflect Thurston's attack. But before he could open his mouth, Birdie spoke up.

"I saw 'em, too, Uncle Matt. I was about to say something when Lockridge beat me to it. Appears they've dropped back. There's places to hide and I reckon they don't want to tip their hand."

Thurston glared at his nephew, but with Birdie's added report he accepted Jake's story and came to a decision.

"All right, we'll veer off and take a different way back so we don't run into 'em. There'll be time enough later to deal with that puffed-up German."

When no one was looking, Jake caught Birdie's eye and gave him a slight nod of thanks. The boy had saved a lot of lives that day. But it wasn't over. Not by a long shot. They were headed for Piedmont and the sheriff had seen him in the role of the hangman. True, their meeting had been brief and Jake had been spiffed up and clean-shaven. but would a pulled-down hat, a scruffy beard, and the old clothes that he wore be an adequate disguise?

Come nightfall Thurston gave the order to stop and make camp. When Jake was off a ways from the others and wrapped in his blankets, he wondered what the coming day would bring. When he finally dropped off, his sleep was fitful. Shortly after dawn, they were on their way again.

"There ain't no sense in all of us riding into town," said Thurston long before they caught sight of Piedmont. "We'll split up and most of you can go on back to the ranch and get to work. All I need to do is see if that bone-head Gillaspy has come up with any leads. But I want some of you with me. A show of power serves to keep folks respectful."

Jake said a silent prayer that he wouldn't be chosen. Thurston reined up and looked them over.

"Ben, I want you and Thad to go with me. You, too, Birdie. And Hogue and Lockridge. The rest of you ride on back to the ranch."

Jake's prayer had gone unanswered. He was headed for Piedmont.

It was well past dark when Decker rode up to the adobe shack. He'd pushed the gelding as hard as he'd dared.

"Hello the house!" he called as he slid out of the saddle.

Tidwell appeared in the doorway, rifle in hand. "What's got you into such a lather, my friend?"

"We've got trouble."

He went inside where enough moonlight filtered in to see. Miguel and Chung Li were awake.

"Gillaspy is going to hang Walkenshaw," he said. "He threw him in jail and set the hanging for day after tomorrow. It's all my fault."

He heard Miguel's swift intake of breath.

"What, no trial?" said Tidwell.

"No."

"What's he supposed to have done?"

"Nothing really. I wrote an editorial. Made two copies and nailed them up in places where they were sure to be read. It raised a lot of questions about the murder and the trial. People were reading it and talking to one another. Gillaspy found out and didn't like it."

"What's that got to do with Walkenshaw?" said Miguel.

"Gillaspy is blaming those editorials on him. He knows Walkenshaw isn't responsible because it isn't his handwriting. But he wants to throw a scare into the townspeople before they can organize and oust him."

"I see," said Tidwell. "As the boss is always saying, defend with a strong attack. Walkenshaw ain't nothing more than a scapegoat."

"That's the size of it. I left town because Gillaspy was searching the hotel. My writing materials were hidden there. But that was before I knew about Walkenshaw. Before Gillaspy jailed him."

"How did you come to find out, being as you were already gone?"

"The young lady who plays the piano at the Vulture's Nest sneaked out of town and rode after me. She's a friend of Walkenshaw's daughter. She's also the niece of the hotel owner. So far as she knows, Gillaspy never found my ink and paper."

"I know the one you're talking about," said Tidwell. "Her name's Montclaire. Pretty girl, and she sure knows how to tickle those ivories."

"She's got a lot of spunk too."

"What are we going to do?" asked Miguel, who'd begun to pace the length of the room. "He helped to save my life. We can't let him hang."

"Agreed," said Decker. "Gillaspy has shown the townspeople exactly what he is—a ruthless outlaw.

"Then I expect that you and me and Chung Li had best ride into town and see what we can do to stop this hanging," said Tidwell.

Miguel bristled. "And why not me?"

Decker spoke up. "Because, amigo, you're the one that started this. Gillaspy would a lot rather have you than Walkenshaw. Might even be using Walkenshaw as bait to draw you in."

"Well, we can't afford to stand around here all night jawin'," said Tidwell. "We'd best get ready to ride."

Decker pulled the saddle from his spent horse and threw it across the back of a fresh mount, a black with a blaze. When he'd finished, the others were waiting, all except Miguel who was being left behind.

"You have to lay low, Miguel," he said. "Keep the horses hid and don't send up any smoke."

The kid was touchy. "I'm not a greenhorn. I know what to do. Just save my friend."

Decker kept forgetting that in spite of his youth, Miguel had been down the trail and over the mountain. He'd do. As for saving Walkenshaw, he wasn't so confident. But they had to try. Gillaspy had a stranglehold on the whole town. The ones who'd supported him must now see his true colors. But they couldn't be depended on to help. Fear and intimidation were powerful weapons, and men like Gillaspy and Thurston wielded them well.

Already tired from his long ride and from staying up the night before, Decker was almost asleep in the saddle when they stopped at dawn. It was now the day before Walkenshaw was to hang.

Tidwell and Chung Li were both familiar with the area.

"There," said Tidwell, pointing to a gentle rise that lay between them and the town. "We'll approach from the north. That way, they're not apt to see us coming."

Decker agreed. At the base of the rise, on the side away from Piedmont, they made a cold camp.

"Best you get some sleep," said Chung Li.

Even though he wasn't accustomed to sleeping in the daytime, Decker didn't need a second invitation. After a couple of hours, Chung Li shook him awake.

"It is time," he said.

It was midmorning.

"One of us ought to take a look from the top of the rise before we go riding down there," said Tidwell.

Decker agreed. "Good idea. I'll go. Wait here."

He pulled a pair of field glasses, a gift from his grandfather, from his saddlebag. Then he made his way to the top on foot, crawling the last few yards. Belly-down, he surveyed the town. Sunlight glinted off the brass fixtures of a buggy that was parked in front of the General Merchandise. Although the town wasn't exactly bustling, several citizens were going about their business. The gallows still stood, a stark reminder of power gone mad. He looked beyond the town and saw riders approaching from the east—six of them. He recognized the blood bay and the rider in its saddle.

"Well, well," he said. "This is going to be interesting."

He scrambled back down to where the others waited.

"See anything?" asked Tidwell.

"The old bull of the herd is coming into town with five of his men. One of 'em is Jake."

"Do tell. With Lockridge on our side, that's four

against five. But then you've got to add Gillaspy and them deputies of his."

"I think it is not good odds," said Chung Li.

Decker felt sorry for him. "Look, I know your boss sent you to us as a messenger. If you want to leave, there won't be any shame in it."

Chung Li grinned. "I think I stay. I have no liking for Thurston, either."

"Good man. Maybe we'd better drift into town one at a time. Might not be noticed that way."

Tidwell and Chung Li had both been seen in town and would certainly be recognized. But the vigilantes and the sheriff would have other things on their minds. They weren't likely to be suspicious of two cowhands bent on some fun. As for himself, Decker looked a lot more disreputable than when he'd been in Piedmont before. Besides, he doubted if Gillaspy had seen him first hand, and he knew that Thurston hadn't.

"I'll go first," he said. "Then Chung Li. Then you, Tidwell."

No one noticed as he tied his horse in an alley behind the grain and feed store. Then he stood in the narrow space between businesses and watched as the Thurston outfit rode into town like they owned the place. He managed to catch Jake's attention. But his friend gave no sign of recognition. They pulled up in front of the jail, right next to the gallows. Decker could hear them talking.

"I could sure use a drink," said the one who was dandied up in new clothes and toting a gun with fancy pearl grips.

"Then go get one," said Thurston, "while me and Conrad have a talk with the sheriff."

While the others headed for the Vulture's Nest, Jake made like he was going to the Whiskey Barrel next door to where Decker was lurking. At the last minute, he sidestepped and joined Decker in the open space. So as not to be seen together, they went single file to the alley.

"Find out anything?" asked Decker.

"Only that Thurston is a cold-blooded snake. But then I had a good idea about that already. He was going to kill all of Santos' people and burn their village."

Decker felt a chill, like somebody had walked on his grave.

"What stopped him?"

"A story that the nephew, Birdie, made up about General Crook patrolling this area after the massacre."

"Good for him. At least somebody in that outfit has a conscience."

"He pulled my irons out of the fire too. They were going to attack the Gebhart place and burn it. I told 'em we were being followed, probably by some of Geb-hardt's powerful friends."

"He buy that?"

"Not until Birdie confirmed it. I owe that kid a lot."

"So the old bull backed off twice. And it was the same places he was run off of before."

"Yeah. He's not a happy fellow. I've got a feeling that somebody is going to get hurt."

Decker looked down at his boots. "I'm afraid that's why I came back. Gillaspy jailed Walkenshaw and claims he's going to hang him in the morning."

"Just like that? What for?"

"To teach the citizens of Piedmont a lesson, I expect. You see, I wrote an editorial and nailed it up in a couple of places. The people were reading it and asking questions about Gillaspy's fitness to be sheriff. I headed out of town when he started searching the hotel. Figured he'd find my paper and stuff."

"Where'd you hide 'em?"

"In the chamber pot."

He watched as the corners of Jake's mouth threatened to turn up. "I can just see old Gillaspy poking around in all those hotel thunder mugs. Maybe he passed 'em by."

"Could be," said Decker. "But he's still got Walkenshaw to hang."

"Where's Miguel?"

"At the adobe. Tidwell and Chung Li are with me. They were going to drift into town one at a time."

He could tell that Jake didn't like the idea of his brother-in-law being left alone at the hideout, but there was no help for it.

"Maybe we ought to slip away and talk to Walkenshaw's daughter," he said. "She'll be plenty worried."

"I expect you're right," said Jake. "I'm plenty worried myself."

He glanced over at the Vulture's Nest. Thurston's men were still occupied, and Thurston and Conrad hadn't come out of the jail.

"Let's be quick about this," he said.

On the edge of town, they stopped across the street from the Walkenshaw house. Decker dismounted and made a pretense of looking at his horse's hoof. From the corner of his eye, he saw a curtain move. Someone was watching at the window. A moment passed before Emily Montclaire came outside and crossed the street.

"I'm certainly glad to see you're a man of your word, Mr. Decker," she said, her expression grave.

He nodded toward Jake. "This is my friend, Jake Lockridge."

She looked him over with one cool glance. Evidently he passed muster.

"I'm glad you're here, Mr. Lockridge. But there's only two of you."

"There's more," said Decker, not mentioning the number since he was sure it would disappoint her. "The others will be drifting in soon, if they haven't already."

"May I ask how many there are?"

There it was. But he couldn't lie. "Two. That'll make four of us altogether."

Decker watched her expression of hope turn to despair.

"Look, it's better than nothing," he said. "Besides, I've got a feeling we won't have any problems with the townspeople. Most of 'em would be glad to run that crooked sheriff clean out of Arizona."

Beyond, at the window, he caught a glimpse of Maybelle Walkenshaw. She was watching them.

"You'd better go, Miss Montclaire," he said. "Tell your friend that we'll do everything we can. Gillaspy isn't going to have the easy time of it that he expects."

"Thank you more than I can say," she said. "I only hope that four of you will be enough."

Having said her piece, she hurried back across the street.

"Are you going to join Thurston's boys again?" asked Decker.

"I figure I'd better. Best way to keep track of 'em. I've got a feeling the old man isn't going to like Gillaspy taking matters into his own hands. He's supposed to follow orders."

"Before you do, we'd better find Tidwell and Chung Li."

It wasn't hard. They were at the livery barn. From there, Chung Li was keeping an eye on the jail.

"Word is that Gillaspy is camping out there until Walkenshaw is hung," said Tidwell. "He doesn't want any more slipups."

"Anybody with him besides Thurston?" asked Decker.

"One of his three deputies."

Decker wasn't surprised. He knew that Gillaspy couldn't afford to look the fool again. Still, it was going to make it harder to spring Walkenshaw.

"The townspeople aren't happy about the way the town's been taken over," he said. "It's possible that some of them might back us when we make our move."

Still, he wasn't counting on it. The way he figured it, if they'd been going to make a stand, they'd have done it a long time ago. But then again, Gillaspy may have gone too far with Walkenshaw's arrest. Way too far.

Chapter Ten

Gillaspy leaned back in his chair, hoisted his booted feet to the desktop, and treated himself to a cigar. He'd managed to get rid of Thurston and his *segundo* quicker than usual, but not without a full measure of the old man's insults. The handwritten reward posters that Thurston's sons had nailed up on their last sashay through town had brought no response at all. No fault of his, but Thurston had made him the target for blame. It didn't help that Thurston's second manhunt was a failure too. One day soon, he promised himself, he'd tell that two-bit rancher where he could go.

The tension from the meeting was draining away when the door opened and the members of the local Citizen's Committee filed in. It was made up of Banker Barstow; Tom Grady from the hotel; Gunter Schmidt, owner of the Whiskey Barrel; and Judge Abel Lowe, the biggest drunk in Arizona Territory. Gillaspy's feet hit the floor and he glared at the committee. Whatever was on their minds meant trouble.

"What do you four want?" he demanded.

"We have to talk," said Barstow.

Gillaspy stood and stretched to his full height of five and a half feet.

"Do you think I've got the time to listen to your whining complaints?" he blustered. "I have more important things to take care of."

"Like what?" asked Barstow with undisguised disgust. "Like sitting there on your backside?"

"Or lynching Walkenshaw without a trial," said Grady. "A man who hasn't done a thing against the law."

"So that's what this is all about. Well, you're wasting your time."

"You're aware that hanging Russ will make you a murderer," chimed in Schmidt. "You'll hang too. Sure as sin. The good people of Piedmont will string you up higher than the biblical Hamon."

Gillaspy slammed his hand on the desk

"Enough of this!" he yelled. "This is my town and I'll run it as I see fit. What's more, I dare any of you to call in outside help."

"You're a criminal," accused the judge. "What's more, I don't for a minute believe that the Sandoval boy was guilty."

"Look here, Judge, you're the one who presided over the trial," Gillaspy reminded him.

"Well, not so as I can remember any of it. I think that getting me drunk was Thurston's doing. Or perhaps it was yours."

"Russ Walkenshaw is a good friend to all of us," said Schmidt. "He's done nothing to be arrested for. The whole town is going to back him."

A finger of fear crept up Gillaspy's spine. He'd had enough. "Wilcox!" he shouted. "Get in here!"

A tough-looking deputy entered from the back room, gun drawn. Gillaspy drew his .45 as well. Judge Lowe took a step back, an expression of horror on his lined face.

"What's the meaning of this outrage?" he said. "We're law-abiding citizens."

"You can't get away with this," said Barstow.

Gillaspy thumbed back the hammer.

"Now, Sheriff, don't go doing something you'll regret," said Schmidt.

Gillaspy looked him in the eye. "I wouldn't regret shooting a mouthy barkeep like you. Or any of you. Now, get out of here. You can spread the word that if anyone tries to spring Walkenshaw, he's going to be shot on sight."

The four of them stared at him like he was a rabid animal. Then they turned and scurried for the door. This struck Gillaspy as comical. He laughed a deep belly laugh. No longer fearful, he felt secure at last in his own power.

"Is Walkenshaw behaving himself?" he asked Wilcox as the deputy was about to return to his station.

"Yeah. Not a peep out of him."

"Since he's the cause of all my troubles, I think I'll look in on him."

He went down the hall to the only occupied cell. His

former deputy was sitting on a cot, elbows on his knees, resting his head in his hands.

"Well it won't be long now," Gillaspy taunted.

Walkenshaw looked up. "Don't know why my hide is so important to you, or why you want to leave my daughter without kith or kin."

"Because you're a worthless old man who's brought me nothing but trouble. You couldn't do a simple job like guarding one dumb kid."

He fixed Gillaspy with a stare. "Now, Gordon, we both know that's not a hanging offense. We also know that the Sandoval kid didn't rob and kill Wade Thurston."

"Are you calling Ben a liar?"

"I sure ain't the first fellow to do that."

"All right, then who did kill Wade? Not that it matters."

"It never did. The old man wanted a scapegoat, not the real killer. But it's plain that one of the Thurston outfit shot him. Had to. Other than Sandoval, who's innocent and didn't have the stolen money, they were the only ones around."

Gillaspy scoffed. "Now, why would someone kill their own kin?"

"I can think of several reasons. And I suspect the old man has thought of them too. He's scared witless that one of his boys killed their brother. Hanging Sandoval puts an end to it. He can fool himself into believing his boys are innocent."

"Now, what reason could any of them boys have to kill Wade?"

"Jealousy over a lady friend, maybe. Or their pa's

favor. Or maybe a flare-up of anger. Who knows but the killer."

Gillaspy mulled that over.

"Well, if anybody wants a quick bullet in the gut, all he has to do is tell that hair-brained theory to Thurston."

Walkenshaw gave him a scathing look. "A man like you don't care nothin' about justice. You're just a killer with a badge."

Gillaspy scowled. Trouble with a condemned man who had nothing to lose, he felt free to get uppity with his talk.

"Prattle on while you can, Walkenshaw. I'll be rid of you tomorrow."

With that he left the prisoner to his own company. When it came down to it, everything was about money and power, he told himself. You did what you had to in order to get it and hold on to it. Look at Matt Thurston. With all that wealth and the gun hands to back him, he could do whatever he pleased. People got out of his way. People respected him. That respect was born out of fear, but so what. Much as Thurston angered and annoyed him, Gillaspy had to admit that he wanted to be exactly like him.

Jake left his friends and went over to the Vulture's Nest where Thurston and his boys were still hanging out. At the bar, he ordered a drink and then moved to one of the tables where he sat alone. It didn't take long for this to be noticed. Hogue, who was already well-fortified and feeling his oats, got up and swaggered over. The man smelled like a brewery.

"Guess you think you're too good to drink with the rest of us, Lockridge."

"I enjoy my own company," he replied.

"Well, I figure you need to be cut down a notch or two."

Jake tensed. Hogue was a bully who liked to show off even at the soberest of times and this wasn't one of them. He was itching for a fight and a saloon brawl was something Jake didn't want. It was likely to draw Gillaspy, who might recognize him. But the way it was shaping up, he wasn't going to have a choice.

"All right, Hogue, if you insist on a fight, let's take it outside so we don't bust up the furniture."

But Hogue wanted an audience.

"Ain't nobody out there to watch me beat you to a pulp."

Birdie moved away from the end of the bar and approached the table.

"He's right, Hogue. No sense in wearing out our welcome. Take your fight out back. Anybody who wants to watch can come along."

"Who are you to be giving me orders, you little runt?" he said, his words slurred while spittle dribbled down his chin.

"Better listen to him," said Thurston. "I like coming in here, and if you was to tear up anything, I'd feel obliged to replace it—using your wages."

The threat got through to Hogue's brain.

"Come on, then, Lockridge. That is, if you don't have a yellow streak."

Jake topped Hogue by an inch or two, but his enemy was a lot heavier. He had almost no neck and a long reach. His fists hung at the ends of his sleeves like hams. Sure of his advantage, the bully couldn't wait to get started. Jake kept an eye on him as they made their way to the alley behind the Vulture's Nest. Ben and Birdie followed. So did the rest of the patrons. As soon as they were outside, Jake turned dead-on to face his challenger. But Hogue had jumped the gun. His head was already down and he butted Jake like a billy goat, knocking the wind out of him and throwing him off balance. Jake fell on his back. As Hogue's foot was coming down to stomp him, he rolled aside at the last second. The big man's boot came down on hard-packed earth. The wicked-looking rowel on the back jingled on impact. Jake grabbed his ankle and jerked. There was a loud thud as Hogue hit the ground.

"Get up!" yelled Ben. "Teach Lockridge some respect."

Jake was first on his feet for he was the more agile. Still, Hogue was quick enough. They faced each other, now. Hogue's face was contorted with rage. Jake sucked in a breath of air and prepared for the next move. Hogue swung. Jake ducked underneath. Coming up inside, he smashed his fist into his opponent's face. A stream of blood spurted from Hogue's nose.

Jake was vaguely aware that others had joined the onlookers. It was the man in front of him that he had to watch. Maddened by the sight of his own blood, Hogue began pounding away. Jake felt stab after stab of pain as he retreated under the onslaught.

"Come on, Lockridge," called Ben. "Stand up and fight like a man."

Hogue was having it his own way, now. Jake could scarcely see through one eye and it felt like a rib was broken. The big man was coming for him again. This time, Jake dodged and threw an uppercut to the jaw. The blow stopped Hogue in his tracks. Jake followed up, pounding away at his gut. The man was like a rock. But even a boulder will fall with the right pressure. One last blow to the jaw sent Hogue teetering. Then he hit the ground.

"Get up!" yelled Ben.

It did no good. Hogue was out cold.

For the first time, Jake had a chance to look around at the crowd that had gathered. Thurston stood there with a sour look on his face. His boys didn't look too happy, either. There was no doubt who they were backing. Birdie's face was unreadable. Then he caught sight of Gillaspy standing at the edge. He'd evidently come late. It made Jake almost thankful for the bruises and swelling that altered his appearance.

"Come on," said Birdie. "I'll take you down to the bathhouse so you can get yourself cleaned up."

As Jake followed him away from the bystanders, he heard someone pouring water on Hogue's unconscious form.

"You did real good," said Birdie, once they were away from the others. "I didn't think anybody could take him on and give him a licking that way."

"Well, he asked for it," said Jake.

"Yep. And he got it. Now, you'd best get washed up and let a doctor check your ribs. Go on ahead. I'll fetch your saddlebags."

The bathhouse was warm and it smelled of dampness and lye soap. He arranged for a bath and eased his aching body into the tub of hot water. Eyes closed, he let the tension drain from his muscles. Then he heard a step. He looked up and saw Birdie.

"Guess you've got clean clothes in one of these," he said, letting the saddlebags drop to the floor.

"Obliged," said Jake.

"Uncle Matt is going to spend the night. That means you'll have a chance to see the doctor and rest up before the ride back to the ranch."

"Staying for the hanging, I guess."

Birdie nodded. "It's not right, but there's nothing I can do about it."

Jake remembered how he'd spoke up to save the village and how he'd backed the ploy to save the Gebhardt ranch.

"You're a good man, Roger Byrd. Don't let anyone tell you different."

It must have been the first time Birdie had heard praise like that for he was rendered speechless. He swallowed hard and with a bob of his head, he turned and hurried out the door.

Jake closed his eyes again and tried to think through the haze of pain. What he needed was a plan. Something that might work. But try as he might, nothing came to mind.

Chapter Eleven

Decker and Chung Li watched from the shadows across the street as the blond-headed kid escorted Jake to the bathhouse.

"He doesn't look so good," said Decker. "But I'd best not be seen with him. Maybe you'd better go check on him. Do whatever you can to help."

Chung Li nodded. "He's still able to walk, though. It would seem that he acquitted himself very well."

"It's no surprise to me. Jake Lockridge is too bull-headed to do anything else. I know that for a fact."

After Chung Li slipped away, Decker went to the back of the livery where Tidwell was biding his time. Tidwell looked up.

"Learn anything?" he asked as he got to his feet.

"They're one less man. Jake took care of a big fellow. I think his name is Hogue."

"Glad to hear it. Be gladder when you tell me that he's took care of all the rest."

"Guess he's going to leave some of 'em to us. I sent Chung Li to check on him, but I think I'll go the back way to the bathhouse and try to talk to him myself. Wait here."

Decker hadn't been recognized so far, but it was best to be careful. He took his time, making sure that no one followed. When he got to the back door of the bathhouse, he ran into Chung Li, who was on his way out.

"Your friend will be as good as new in a few days," said Chung Li. "You can go on in. There's no one else inside but the attendant. I'll return to the livery barn and wait with Tidwell."

Decker always liked the way these places smelled. Warm and clean. He found Jake toweling off. The way he braced his rib cage with his arm made it clear that he was in pain. His face was scarcely recognizable, it was so discolored and swollen.

"You ought to see a doctor," said Decker.

"I was planning on it as soon as I get dressed. I need to get these ribs bound up. When the doc is through, I'll head your way."

"Look, I know you need attention," said Decker, "but it's important that I talk to you before you go."

Jake hurriedly pulled on his clothes. "All right," he said glancing over at the attendant. "Let's step out back where it's a little more private."

Outside, they appeared to be alone, but Decker stepped close and spoke in a low voice.

"I've got a hunch about who shot Wade Thurston and

robbed him," he said. "I heard at the mercantile that the fellow you just whipped has been spending a lot of money. More than any thirty-a-month cowhand ought to have. He hasn't been in town to gamble, either, so he didn't come by it that way."

Jake nodded. "It seems we're on the same track. I've been wondering about his fancy gun and expensive new clothes myself."

"I thought you said you suspected one of the brothers."

"I do. But Hogue's mixed up in this somehow. Maybe he saw something and the killer is paying him off."

It sounded plausible to Decker. "It could be any of three remaining brothers, I guess."

"True," said Jake. "But my vote still goes to Ben. After all, he was the one who lied at the trial. And he's said to have a bad temper once he's riled."

"So now all we've got to do is prove it."

"Ryan," said Jake, "you've got a real knack at getting to the heart of things. Now, let me get myself over to the doctor's place. I'll meet you at the livery barn when he's done."

"I expect you'll be sore for a while," said Doc Hatcher after he'd bound Jake's ribs and doctored his cuts. "A couple of your ribs were cracked, but you're real lucky. The man who cracked them is in the other room. He's in lots worse shape than you, which I wouldn't have predicted, hefty as he is. You must have learned how to fight somewhere along the line."

"My uncle taught me. But I want you to know I

didn't start that fight. Hogue did. There was no way to avoid it."

"It doesn't appear to have been his smartest move. Next time maybe he'll think twice before he starts swinging."

Jake paid him for his services, shouldered his saddlebags, and headed down the alley toward the stable to join the others. Decker was in the back with Tidwell and Chung Li. The hostler was out front, well out of earshot and minding his own business.

Tidwell wore a look of concern.

"When we try to spring Walkenshaw, we'll be going up against the Thurstons and they're backed by Gillaspy and his three deputies."

"It won't be quite so bad now," said Decker. "After the beating Jake gave Hogue, he's going to be laid up for a while."

"I don't think they can count on the nephew, either," said Jake. "He despises the things his uncle does. He won't try to stop us. Fact is, I have a feeling he'd join us if he could."

Tidwell did some mental arithmetic and appeared to be a little more cheerful, but not much.

"If you're right," he said, "then it's down to seven against four."

"Maybe we can add another man to our side," said Decker. "The woman who plays the piano at the Vulture's Nest is the niece of the hotel owner. According to her, he's fed up with Gillaspy and the ones that are keeping him in office. I think he'd join us if we were to ask. His name is Tom Grady."

"Can you talk to him without being seen?" said Jake. "The more we even the odds, the better."

"I'll try. Then too, he might know of others who would join us. While I'm gone, you'd better try to get some rest."

The way Jake felt, he needed it and wasn't about to argue the matter.

While Decker went to the hotel to enlist Grady's help, Jake bedded down in the hay. Chung Li and Tidwell were left to keep watch.

It seemed like he'd just dozed off when he heard the sound of a woman's strident voice.

"I insist on seeing whoever is in charge," she said. "It's my father's life that's at stake and I refuse to stand by and do nothing."

She was more than Tidwell could handle. "Lockridge," he said, "we've got trouble."

Jake painfully got to his feet. He needed to shut her up before she attracted unwanted attention.

"Miss Walkenshaw," he said. "You ought not to be here."

Her trim figure was clad in a tan riding outfit and her face wore an expression of grim determination.

"You're going to save my father," she said, "and I'm going to help you."

"Now, how do you plan to do that?" he asked.

She pulled a pistol from her waistband. It was a Remington with an octagonal barrel and ivory grips.

"This is fully loaded," she said. "What's more, I know how to use it. Nothing would give me greater pleasure than to put a bullet between that little toad's eyes."

"By that, I presume you mean Gillaspy."

She gave him a withering look that made him glad he wasn't the toad she was after.

"Miss, we're only going to have one chance," he said. "This has to be done right."

"Just so long as I'm in on it."

He had to admire her spunk. In a way, she reminded him of Alicia, a woman who had plenty of her own.

"We're going to have to make our move when they're bringing him out to the scaffold. There's no way we can spring him from the jail without getting him killed. I doubt if any of the townspeople will interfere. That means there's likely to be four of us against several of the enemy."

He saw a glint of determination in her eyes.

"Whether you like it or not, Mr. Lockridge, I'm in. You can change that number to five. And you're right about the townspeople. They're outraged with Gillaspy and that whole kit and kaboodle of Thurstons. There's talk that Gillaspy is half mad and they're afraid that my father won't be the last to face the gallows. It's just that they have families and they're afraid. But once you make your move, some of them may join us. At least they won't hinder us."

Jake knew human nature all too well. It was easy to sit back and let others do the hard work and take the risks. Regardless, he didn't want Maybelle Walkenshaw in the line of fire. He was about lay down the law and send her home, but it occurred to him that she might go off and do something foolish on her own. Better to have her with them, he decided, than out messing things up and getting herself or her father killed.

"All right," he agreed. "But you'll follow orders and you'll stay out of sight until it's time for us to make our move."

Her expression changed to one of gratitude. "You won't be sorry," she promised.

He already was.

"We're going to be in position when they bring him out in the morning. You're to be waiting at your house, ready to ride. We may have to make a run for it. Pack what food you can. This is apt to be a long haul."

"Thank you," she said simply. Then she opened the door and slipped out the way she'd come in.

"I don't like it," said Tidwell who'd been listening. "Things is bad enough without having to look out for some skittish woman on top of everything else."

"It's best that we know where she is. That way, we might be able to keep her safe. We sure don't want Gillaspy getting his hands on her."

"You've got a point there," he conceded. "Still, I don't much like it."

Before Jake could go back to sleep, there was a light tap on the back door. He got up, drew his gun, and stood to one side while Tidwell opened the door. It was Decker.

"Get inside before someone spots you," Jake ordered.

"Strange," said Decker. "I thought I saw a woman leaving the barn."

"She was here all right," said Tidwell. "It was the Walkenshaw woman and Lockridge let her join up with us."

"Don't say anything," Jake ordered when he saw that Decker was about to protest. "She's going to wait for us and be ready to ride. Best to take her with us, anyway. We can't predict how far Gillaspy would go. Thurston, either. It wouldn't be safe to leave her for them to take hostage."

Decker agreed. "You're right, of course. By the way, I talked to Tom Grady. He's with us. He was in the war and knows how to shoot. Gunter Schmidt, who owns the Whiskey Barrel, is with us too. Grady steered me to him. They don't quite trust the banker, though. Grady said that a strong breeze could make Barstow flutter in a different direction. They don't dare let the judge in on this, either. He hates Thurston and Gillaspy, but with his addiction to drink, he's not dependable."

"Nice work," said Jake. "The odds are starting to even up a little more. We'll take our positions before sunup and get the jump on 'em when they bring their prisoner from the jail."

"Where do you want us to be?"

"I'm going to be in the space between buildings near the sheriff's office. I want someone posted on the other side of the jail, and a man stationed on the roof across the street with a shotgun. Someone needs to have the horses ready since we'll have to make a run for it. We'll pick up Miss Walkenshaw on our way out of town."

It was decided that Tidwell would be on the roof and Chung Li would hold the horses in readiness. Decker would be on the other side of the jail. When their plan was complete, Jake went back to sleep.

* * *

Inside the Vulture's Nest Thurston had made himself comfortable at one of the tables where he sat nursing a glass of beer. He congratulated himself on not having bet on the fight. He'd been sure that Hogue could whip Lockridge easy. After all, he was beefy and strong and he'd bragged about all the fights he'd won. Still, he lost.

There was something about Lockridge that bothered him. Maybe it was that quiet self-assurance that bordered on arrogance. Somehow, he didn't have the manner of an ordinary saddle tramp. No doubt there was more to the man than met the eye.

"We're all staying for the hanging, ain't we, Pa?" asked Thad who sat across the table, slopping beer down his shirtfront.

"I said we was, didn't I."

"I reckon that no-account deputy deserves to have his neck stretched, Pa. But won't his friends try to stop it?"

Thurston wiped beer foam from his mouth.

"I doubt it," he said. "What friends he's got are a bunch of yellow bellies. Gillaspy's put the scare in 'em."

"Little brother, we're going to stay right here and see that everything goes exactly the way it's supposed to," said Ben, who'd come up behind Thad. "It's time we let everybody know who's the boss around here."

"It appears to me that Gillaspy thinks he's the boss," said Thad. "But you are, ain't you, Pa."

"Yes, and don't you forget it."

"Are they going to bring Walkenshaw out come daylight?" he asked.

"Yeah. Same as usual."

"But there ain't no proper hangman. Who's going to do it?"

"There can't be that much to hanging a fellow," said Thurston. "If Gillaspy ain't got the stomach, I'll do it myself."

Thurston saw the look of admiration on his son's face. The boy had the least wits of all his offspring, but he was the easiest to impress.

"We'll take turns standing guard at the jail tonight. If anybody's going to try to spring the prisoner, it'll be under the cover of darkness, just like Sandoval was sprung."

"That's Gillaspy's job," Ben complained, "and he's got deputies to help."

Thurston frowned at him. "I don't care," he said. "We're doubling the guard and having someone patrol the street. Anybody who tries to break into that jail is a dead man."

"Then there's no doubt about it," said Thad, a look of pleasure on his face. "We're having ourselves a hanging."

Thurston leaned across the table and swatted him with his hat.

"Shut up and show some respect, boy. This is business. Something that's got to be done. It ain't pleasure. Leastwise not with Walkenshaw. Might have been with your brother's killer."

Chastened, Thad got up and went to the bar to order another beer.

Thurston glanced at his back and sighed. Thad was his son, same as Ben and Gabe, but he could be a trial.

He'd been Viola's last baby and there simply hadn't been enough brains to go around.

He downed the last of his drink and shoved his chair back.

"It's best I get over to the jail," he said. "I need to tell Gillaspy what's what. Soon as it gets dark, Ben, I want you to patrol the street. If anyone's outside, tell 'em to get. If they give you any trouble, pistol-whip 'em. If that don't work, shoot 'em. I'll have Thad relieve you around midnight."

"Right, Pa. Better tell that to my brother before he gets too drunk to see straight."

"You tell him. And bring him along. He can sleep in the jail until it's time for him to go on duty."

Thurston knew that Gillaspy resented him horning in. But without his backing, Gillaspy was nothing but a cow thief with a running iron. It was best to show him who was boss from time to time. It was a good thing to show this sorry excuse for a town too.

When he entered the jail, the sheriff looked up from the paperwork on his desk.

"That was quite a fight out back of the saloon," he said. "I saw a little of it, but I was afraid it might be a diversion for a jailbreak so I figured I'd better get back here and keep an eye on things."

"Smart move," said Thurston. "But my man, Hogue, started it. Lockridge finished it."

"Is Hogue all right?"

"Can't say that I care. Anyhow, he's over at the doc's office."

"What about the other fellow?"

"My nephew took him over to the bathhouse. Haven't seen him since. Might have been hurt worse than we thought."

"Guess we can't count on either of them for any help." It sounded like an accusation and Thurston took it as one.

"You can count on me and my two sons. I suppose my nephew might be called on, if need be."

"Never mind," said Gillaspy. "I expect me and my men can handle it. I won't be needing any of you."

His tone and manner were way too uppity for Thurston to let pass.

"I've heard that before," he said. "Seems to me it was right before my son's killer escaped."

Gillaspy's face turned a bright shade of red. Thurston kept his hand close to his revolver, prepared for whatever might come. But Gillaspy held his temper.

"Wasn't my fault. But on second thought, I'll take the extra help. Still, nobody in their right mind would try to break Walkenshaw out tonight. Come morning, he'll serve as a warning to anybody else who's got a mind to cross me—or you."

Thurston smiled, knowing how much pain that little speech had cost.

"I'll see you bright and early tomorrow morning, then," he said. "Sleep lightly."

He overheard Gillaspy's muttered curse as he closed the door. It brought a smile to his face.

Chapter Twelve

Jake was awake before daylight. He lay still for a few minutes, thinking of the task that lay ahead. Then leaving the warmth of his blankets he prepared himself. He pulled on his boots, then belted the .44 around his waist. Next, he took a knife from one of his saddlebags and stuck it under his belt. A night's rest had restored him more than he'd hoped. He touched his face. The swelling had gone down. The bound ribs would cause no problem.

Tidwell was awake and struggling to get ready in the dim light.

"Guess it's time, Lockridge."

"Looks like. I'm counting on you, Tidwell. And whatever you do, don't fall off the roof."

"I'll do my best. Where are you going to put them fellows from town?"

"Grady, behind the front door of his hotel. Schmidt,

133

just inside his saloon. Decker was to tell them. Since both places are across the street from the gallows, they'll have a clear shot."

Chung Li was readying the horses by the light of a lantern when a footfall warned of someone outside. There was a tapping on the door. Jake opened it to let Decker, Grady, and Schmidt file in. They were followed by Maybelle Walkenshaw, who was dressed like a man, her hair hidden by a hat. He wasn't pleased to see her.

"I thought I told you to stay home and be ready to ride," he said.

She glared at him. "Come what may, my place is here with the rest of you."

He started to make a sharp reply, then relented. "All right, you can help Chung Li with the horses."

To his surprise, she obeyed without argument.

Now that everyone was present, Jake went over the plan again.

"Chung Li, you and Miss Walkenshaw are to bring the horses to the alley near the jail a few at a time. Then keep them out of sight behind that old storehouse. The rest of us will split up, take our places, and keep alert. Gillaspy is sure to have at least one deputy watching the streets until it's time for the big show."

"I spotted him," said Decker. "I also saw one of the Thurston boys down at the other end of town. Seems they're not taking any chances."

Jake pulled out his pocket watch and glanced at it in the lantern light. "As soon as people begin to stir around out there we'll get started. We need to be ready when the prisoner is brought out."

"Understood," said Chung Li. "But what of the men on the street who are watching?"

"You'd best wait until there's some wagon traffic and horses. That way, you won't be noticed. And don't go near the jail until you're out of sight in the alley. Now, we need to leave before the hostler arrives."

"I'm acquainted with him," said Maybelle. "He's my father's friend. He won't trouble us."

Schmidt and Grady were the first to leave for their respective hiding places. Decker and Tidwell followed. He started to tell Chung Li to snuff the lantern, but the man anticipated his order and the livery stable went dark.

It was Jake's turn. Outside, the town was still swathed in predawn gray. The air was crisp and cold. Jake drew a deep breath, hoping this morning wouldn't be the last he'd ever see. He eased the door shut behind him and took a step. Across the alleyway, a shadow moved. He tensed. His hand went to the knife in his belt for a gunshot would alert his enemies. With a quick motion, he pulled it out.

"Put that thing away!" a voice hissed. "It's me. Your brother."

Jake nearly dropped the knife.

"Miguel? What are you doing here? Why aren't you back at the hideout?"

"It was no longer healthy to stay there. Yesterday, a small band of Apaches came close. Too close. Lucky for me, they were herding cows and not hunting white-eyes. But I couldn't risk having them come back and find me. As soon as it got dark, I packed up and headed for town."

The renegades must have helped themselves to a rancher's cattle. Jake admitted that dangerous as it was for Miguel to be in town, he'd made the right choice. Still, he may have jumped from the skillet into the campfire.

"Come over here," he said in a voice little louder than a whisper. "You need to know what we're planning to do."

Quickly, Jake filled him in.

"Glad I came to town. I can help."

"You'll be a big help if you'll stay out of sight. I don't want them to get their hands on you. We'd end up exchanging one condemned man for another."

"Don't worry. I have your Uncle Nate's pistol and plenty of ammunition."

That didn't make him feel any better. Miguel was impulsive. He'd jumped the gun once before when they were attacked by Culebra's outlaws. True, he had been younger, then. But Jake didn't want that happening again.

"Stay behind me and back me up," he said.

"Now, you're talking. I'll stick right with you."

At this early hour, the saloons had their doors closed. Gone were the noises of revelry, along with the sounds of classical music. There were a few wagons on the street and there would soon be more. There were horses too. Chung Li wouldn't be noticed. Neither would Maybelle, thanks to her disguise.

From where he lurked at the side of the livery barn, he had a good view of the entire street. He spotted one of the guards. He was leaning against the front wall of the jail, having a smoke. Then he heard the clomp and jingle of boots on the boardwalk. It was growing lighter and he could see that it was Thurston himself. When the smoker left his place and started moving toward the far end of town, Jake held his breath, willing Thurston to go in the opposite direction. Instead, he paused and stood sniffing the air like an old hound dog. Jake reached down and groped along the ground until his fingers closed over a rock. Then from cover, he hurled the stone toward the far end of the street. It landed with a thud on the wooden sidewalk, causing Thurston to jump and grab for iron. Not seeing anyone, the rancher went to investigate.

"Now," he whispered to Miguel.

They slipped across the street, silent as wraiths, and concealed themselves in a narrow space between buildings.

"What's going on?" asked the deputy, who spotted Thurston squatting on his haunches, studying an ordinary rock.

"Don't know," he said. "But I don't like it. Looks like somebody throwed this thing."

"Didn't hit you did it?"

"Nope. I guess Walkenshaw still has some friends around who want to stir up trouble, even if it's something as silly as this."

"Well, I don't reckon it's anything to worry about. It's cold out here. I'm going back to the jail and warm up a mite."

"I think I'll go with you," said Thurston. "Maybe I can find something in Gillaspy's cupboard to warm my insides."

The deputy chuckled. "I know right where it is."

They both moved on down the street and entered the jail. Jake let out the breath he'd been holding. Now all they had to do was wait.

A wagon drawn by two mules clattered down the street. It was soon followed by another. Maybelle brought out a couple of horses and made her way across to the alley. A few minutes passed before Chung Li made his second trip. They were doing well.

When streaks of dawn finally appeared over the eastern mountains, every nerve in Jake's body was alert. They should all be in place, now. He looked up at the roof opposite, trying to catch a glimpse of Tidwell. The man was well hidden.

Each minute that ticked by seemed like an hour. Down the street, at the Vulture's Nest, the swamper came out and swept the debris off the walkway in front. Another half-dozen riders were added to the wagon traffic.

While Jake watched, the mercantile opened and so did the grain and feed store. To his right, he saw a man in a broadcloth suit unlock the front door of the undertaker's establishment. A cold chill ran down his spine. No doubt the man expected his services to be needed soon. He wondered why men who dealt with the dead always looked humorless and undernourished.

He caught sight, then, of the two Thurston brothers coming from the hotel. Putting a finger to his lips for silence, he shoved Miguel deeper into the space that hid them. He pressed his own back against the wall so he couldn't be seen. It appeared the enemy was gathering.

Miguel tugged at his arm and he turned to see Maybelle gesturing from the alley.

"What is it?" he said when he reached her.

"I just wanted you to know that the horses are in place, ready to go. I knew you'd be concerned."

"Fine," he said. He'd been watching from his place of concealment and already knew this was so. "Go stay with them. This is apt to get ugly."

In spite of the fear in her eyes, she was poised. Without another word she turned and hurried back to Chung Li.

It would soon be time to bring out Walkenshaw. In spite of the fact he was well-liked, a crowd had begun to form. Not all of them had come to gawk, he was sure. Some of them must be there to pray for a miracle.

It was then that he heard Gillaspy's booming voice as the jailhouse door opened.

"It's going to be a fine day for a hanging, my friends. There's not a cloud in the sky."

Jake's hand went to the grips of the .44.

"Look, are you sure you know how to do this?" came a voice that he recognized as Thurston's.

"Trust me," said Gillaspy. "Walkenshaw ain't going to have a single complaint."

Gillaspy chuckled at his feeble joke just as Walkenshaw was brought out by a pair of deputies.

"Up the steps, now," ordered Gillaspy. "Careful. Wouldn't want to you to trip and fall."

Jake could hear it all and he felt the deepest revulsion. The man was half mad.

He glanced up at the roof and saw the barrel of

Tidwell's shotgun. He was waiting for the signal to start and Jake gave it to him. Then he stepped out on the street, gun drawn.

"Cut him loose, Gillaspy!" he yelled. "And the rest of you keep your hands where I can see 'em."

There were gasps from the crowd as they pulled back from the gallows.

Gillaspy found himself looking down the barrel of a Colt. His deputies raised their hands. So did Thurston and his boys. Jake caught a glimpse of Birdie's face and saw on it an expression of relief.

"Now, look here," Gillaspy blustered. "You can't come in here and flout the law like you're doing."

"You're a fine one to talk about flouting the law," said Jake. "The first one of you owlhoots that moves is going to die."

"Knowed I shouldn't have trusted you, Lockridge," said Thurston. His eyes were narrowed, his hatred undisguised.

"You're all alone," said Ben, a smirk on his face. "Do you think we can't take you?"

"He ain't that alone," called Tidwell from the roof. "Remember me, Ben?"

When he saw Tidwell and the shotgun, Ben's smirk was replaced by fear.

Decker appeared on the far side of the gallows, his pistol drawn. "If that's not enough, make it three," he said.

"Folks around here ain't going to let you get away with this," Gillaspy threatened. "They'll hunt you down sure as sin."

"You might be disappointed in them," said Grady as

he stepped out of the hotel armed with a revolver. "It's you and your gunmen that folks are sick of, and Thurston, over there, acting like he's some kind of duke or baron. We're not about to let you murder our friend and hide your crime behind a tin badge."

Schmidt joined him on the street. "Everything my friend, here, said goes for me too."

Gillaspy's cockiness disappeared. He looked scared and desperate. Matt Thurston was livid.

"I won't tell you again to cut Walkenshaw loose," said Jake.

Without Gillaspy's leave to do so, one of the deputies began sawing the prisoner's bonds with a knife.

"Over here beside me," said Jake when Walkenshaw's hands were free.

The scarecrow of a man lumbered over to join him.

"Now, Gillaspy, there's some empty cells inside for you and Thurston and his boys. If you want to live, you'll drop your weapons and head for those cells. Your deputies can leave town, providing they never show their faces in this part of the Territory again."

They hesitated, not wanting to give up. Still they wanted to live.

"Very well," said the dark-bearded deputy with a bandolier across his chest. "I've been wanting to take a ride over to California. Let me go and you'll never see me again."

"It's a deal," said Jake.

On his way to a piebald that was tied to the hitch rail, the former deputy pulled off his badge and dropped it in the dirt. The other two followed him.

"I paid you good money!" yelled Gillaspy. "Come back here and earn it."

"You didn't pay me enough to die," said the one on the piebald. "*Adios.*"

Without another word, the three rode out of town, leaving a cloud of dust behind them.

"Now, the rest of you inside," Jake ordered.

He grabbed the keys from a peg and prodded Gillaspy forward.

"I'm sure you know that the cells are down there," he said.

While he kept them covered, Decker locked them in. All the while they threatened and cursed.

Birdie had followed along, no doubt expecting the same fate as the others. When the cell doors had slammed shut and he was still on the outside, he looked at Jake questioningly. It was plain that he didn't want to be singled out for special treatment in front of his uncle and cousins.

"You," he said, nodding to Birdie. "I've got work for you to do."

"Open this door," said Ben, "and I'll go to work for you."

Jake turned on his heel and left. Decker and Schmidt stayed to guard the cells.

Outside, Birdie asked, "What is it that you want me to do?"

"That piece of junk over there," he said, nodding toward the scaffolding. "I want it torn down. No town should have to look at something like that every day."

"Be glad to. Got some tools?"

"Grady, here, will provide you with whatever you need."

Jake looked over to see Walkenshaw wrapped in the arms of his daughter. Nearby, Miguel was helping Chung Li with the horses. Tidwell had left his perch on the roof and was crossing the street.

"We need to get all of those reward posters down," Jake told him. "Let it be known that there's no price on Miguel's head or anyone else's."

"I'll get it done."

"So what do we do, now?" asked Decker who'd come outside, deciding that Schmidt could handle the guard duty by himself.

"We dispatch a messenger to the capital. Tell them to send a deputy marshal up here, along with a judge who's sober."

Grady was standing nearby, listening. "I'm going to call a special meeting of the city council," he said. "We're going to appoint an interim sheriff until we can hold an election. We want you to take the job, Lockridge."

Jake wasn't wild about the job offer, still he didn't see how he could refuse. The meeting was held, and before nightfall he was wearing a badge. He wondered what Alicia would think about that.

Once Birdie started tearing the scaffolding down, he was joined by a dozen axe-wielding citizens. It was gone in record time. When darkness fell, the townspeople built a bonfire with the wood scraps, and the gathering had all the earmarks of a celebration. You'd have thought they'd stormed the Bastille, Jake thought.

While the rest were celebrating and letting off steam, he turned in. This time he put up in a hotel room. The whooping and singing that drifted up to his window made him feel a deep sense of loneliness. He was far from home and it had been a long time since he'd seen his wife and daughter.

A glance in the mirror showed a reflection that was familiar. Although the bruises remained, the swelling was gone. His body was still sore, but less painful than it had been. The bandage on his ribs had helped considerably. If need be, he could ride.

He'd assigned Decker to watch Birdie. In his opinion, the slight-built, blond-haired young man was a far better person than any of his kinfolk, but trust was something that Jake didn't give lightly.

It was long after he'd gone to sleep that he was yanked to wakefulness by gunshots. They were coming from the direction of the jail. Already dressed, he jammed his feet into his boots and strapped on his pistol. By the time he made it to the street, there was the sound of retreating horses. Someone fired two shots in the dark.

"What happened?" Jake asked the first man he came across.

"Jailbreak. Killed the guard. Stole some horses and took off."

Jake sprinted across to the jail. Inside, a kerosene lamp threw shadows across the walls. The room was filled with the odor of gun smoke. Grady was on his knees beside Tidwell.

"I sent someone to fetch the doctor," said Grady, "but I think it's too late."

Jake squatted on his haunches and placed his hand under Tidwell's nose. No air was going in or out. Blood covered his shirt; blood with a copper smell to it.

"I'm afraid you're right," he said.

"It looks like they got the jump on him and took his gun. You can see his holster is empty."

Miguel was suddenly there, as was Chung Li and Decker.

"I worked with this man a long time," said Chung Li. "He is a good friend and good worker."

"Don't worry," said Jake. "We'll catch the ones that shot him."

"Then I would like to be with you."

Jake nodded. "You will be," he said. "We'll do this together."

The townspeople let their displeasure be known when they heard of the murder and jailbreak. Jake looked for Birdie and found him in his bedroll in a corner of the livery. He claimed that he'd been sleeping until the gunshots woke him up. After that, he'd stayed where he was, fearing his relatives would seek him out.

"They killed Tidwell," Jake told him. "We're going after your uncle and the rest of them."

"I understand," said Birdie. "They did a lot of things I didn't want to be a part of, but I didn't have any choice."

"Did you have any part of their jailbreak?"

"No," he said. "I swear I didn't."

Jake believed him.

"You're to stay here and help Miss Walkenshaw. Don't leave town. I'll bring your uncle and the others back alive if I can. If not, well . . ."

"I know," said Birdie to the unfinished sentence. "Uncle Matt never gave anybody half a chance. Didn't believe in it. Best you don't give him one, either."

Again Jake felt sorry for the orphaned boy who'd been taken in by an outlaw with killer instincts.

"Where's Hogue?" Birdie asked.

"They were bringing him from the doctor's place. He's in good enough shape to be locked up, and nobody wants him out causing more trouble."

"He's another bad one," said Birdie. "Hogue would stick a knife in your back as soon as you turned around."

Jake didn't doubt it. That was what prompted the order to put him behind bars.

At dawn the posse gathered in front of the jail on the spot where the gallows had stood the morning before. Riding with Jake were Decker, Miguel, Chung Li, Grady, and Schmidt. The others had families to protect, as well as the town. He understood. As for the men who made up the posse, he couldn't have asked for better.

"Let's ride," he ordered.

In the early morning light, it was easy to follow the outlaws' trail. It ran east toward the high country. He figured Thurston intended to do what he and Miguel had done when they were being hunted. It was easy to hide in the mountain wilderness.

Separated from his men, Thurston had only his sons, Thad and Ben. Then there was Gillaspy, a man that Thurston would be a fool to trust.

"I was betting they'd head for Thurston's ranch,"

said Decker when they stopped to let the horses rest. "They could've added a lot of gun hands."

"Maybe," said Jake. "Most likely his son, Gabe, would have joined them too. But I suspect that a lot of those men would draw the line at running from the law."

"Might be that Thurston would lie to them."

"No doubt. But it wouldn't take them long to figure out something wasn't right."

"So you think they're going to try to hide in the mountains?"

"That would be my guess."

Miguel stood nearby, looking worried.

"You don't suppose they'll go back to Santos' village and cause trouble, do you?"

Jake shook his head. "If Thurston is dumb enough to show his face around there again, the villagers will make short work of him and his boys."

Miguel looked reassured. "I believe you're right. It's best not to underestimate Señor Santos and his men."

"I figure they have a four-hour head start on us," said Jake. "They've got no spare horses, and I doubt if they have much food or water."

"That means they'll have to find some or steal some," said Decker. "Where is the nearest place?"

"Besides Santos' village? That would be Gebhardt's ranch. Unless Gephardt has an outlying line shack or something of that nature, and I didn't spot one. How about it, Chung Li?"

"There is nothing," he replied. "If they didn't bring water with them when they escaped, they will have to rely on a *tinaja*, a natural gathering tank, and these are very few and far between."

"But they must know we're on their trail," said Decker. "What's to stop them from hiding and lying in wait to ambush us?"

"Nothing at all," said Jake. "Nothing at all."

Chapter Thirteen

Gillaspy's hands shook as he gripped the reins. He'd been looking at a long term in prison until Ben tricked that guard and grabbed his pistol. But then Ben had to go and shoot him. Now, a posse was sure to be on their tail, and they weren't apt to turn back. As it stood, he was looking at worse than prison. If he was caught, he would hang along with the Thurstons.

He hadn't been on the run from the law in a long time. Not since he'd stopped putting brands on other men's cattle, and the easy years had made him soft.

It gave him a measure of satisfaction that Thurston wasn't faring so well, either. Not that you could tell it from his high-and-mighty attitude. Had it been just the two of them, he would have plugged Thurston before they'd reached the outskirts of Piedmont. As it was, the old man was protected by Ben and Thad. Even though Thad was slow-witted, he was fast enough with a pistol.

For now, there was nothing to do but play along. With luck, he'd get his chance later.

They'd retrieved their sidearms before leaving the jail. They'd also helped themselves to the shotguns and rifles that were kept there, along with enough ammunition to fight a fair-size rebellion. If they ran across Apaches, they'd need it. As for the posse, if they caught up, they'd get a hot reception. The only thing lacking was food and water. Food they could provide. Water was another matter.

In their favor, they were making good time. By the first signs of daylight, they'd put a lot of distance between themselves and the town.

"I'm hungry," Thad complained.

"Ain't nothing to eat," said his pa, "and we can't take time to go hunting."

"Do you think some of 'em started after us right away?"

Ben snorted in disgust at his brother's question. "Look over your back trail. Do you see any sign of 'em?"

Thad twisted in his saddle and took a look.

"Nope."

"Then they didn't start right away, else you'd see 'em."

"Oh, I didn't think of that. Where we goin', Pa?"

"To the mountains."

"How come we didn't go back to our ranch? We've got lots of fellas working for us who could've run 'em off as soon as they showed up. Might have even shot 'em for us."

"Stop and think," said Thurston. "That posse would have cornered us there like rats in a barn. You know you can't count on any of them saddle bums that Conrad hired. At the first sign of trouble they'd likely hand us over."

"What about Gabe? He could stop 'em from doing it."

"Gabe can't do nothing. They don't pay attention to him."

Gillaspy wanted to tell Thurston and that dumb kid of his to shut up. They were getting on his nerves. But he didn't dare.

"Pa, why don't we go back to that Mexican village and make 'em give us food and water?" Thad persisted.

"Because there's only four of us and I don't want to get shot full of holes. Now, be quiet. It's time to walk the horses for a while. Have to take care of 'em. They're all we've got."

"But I don't like to walk, Pa."

"Don't matter what you like," said Ben. "Mind what Pa says."

Gillaspy was grateful for the quiet that followed. He needed to work things out in his mind. His life and his future depended on how well he did it.

Sam Conrad stood in his stirrups and gazed into the distance. He was worried. The boss should have been back, by now. But there was nary a sign of a rider, let alone half a dozen. He didn't like it. But then he didn't like a lot that had been happening since Wade's death. Thurston was tore up inside and unpredictable. He was more willing than usual to step beyond the boundaries of he law. On top of that, Piedmont's sorry excuse for a sheriff was making things worse.

Conrad eased back in the saddle and pulled out the makings for a smoke. While he gently tapped tobacco from the pouch into the paper, he thought of his future. There was no denying it, he was getting older. What's more, he sensed that his job wasn't as secure as it once had been. It was the best he'd ever had too. The pay was good. He had authority. And there was a certain amount of prestige that went along with being the foreman of the biggest ranch in this part of the country. One thing for sure, he wasn't going to give it up without a fight. Hogue must have heard something, though, or felt something, for he was like a hound on the heels of a wounded buck. The way he was showing off with a fancy new gun and high-price clothes confirmed it. Where could a thirty-a-month saddle bum have gotten that kind of money? A bonus from Thurston, maybe? He thought of the large sum of money Wade had been carrying. But if that was the source, Thurston must have thought of it too. Or maybe not. He was so wrapped up in his hate that his view was narrow. One thing Conrad knew for certain, it was necessary for a man to look after his own interests. From now on that's exactly what he intended to do.

When he finished his smoke, he'd reached a decision. It was time to act. He wheeled his horse and rode back to the others. Within the hour, half a dozen men were mounted and ready to ride. With one exception, they'd all been hand-picked for loyalty to himself. The exception was Gabe Thurston.

"You really think Pa's in trouble?" said Gabe, his tone skeptical.

"Looks to me like it. He'd have been here if he wasn't."

"Then we're heading for Piedmont?"

"Close by, anyhow. I aim to stop before we get there. It'd be smart to send in a man to nose around. See what's going on. Could save us from riding into trouble."

Gabe smirked. "You're starting to act like an old woman, Conrad. Pa can handle anybody in that town. Him and the boys are having a good time, that's all."

Conrad kept a rein on his temper, but it wasn't easy.

"Gabe, if you've got better things to do, then by all means stay here and do 'em. I'll make sure and tell your pa when we find him."

The threat worked.

"Oh, I believe I'll come along," said Gabe. "I want to see the look on your face when Pa fires you. He's been planning on doing that for a long time, now."

Conrad recoiled as if he'd been slapped in the face. It was a brazen attack on his authority, an attempt to humiliate him in front of the men. He managed to keep his voice devoid of emotion.

"Suit yourself. Let's get moving. We're burning daylight."

It was dark when they reined up within sight of the town lights. Conrad spoke to Shorty, a man he trusted more than the others.

"I want you ride into town, scout around. See if you can find Mr. Thurston or any of the boys. If not, then try to find out what's happened to 'em. Then get back here on the double."

"Right, boss, I'll do 'er."

Shorty was dependable. In his favor, too, was the fact

that he was a nondescript little man who was easy to overlook. The perfect spy.

Meanwhile, the rest of them filled their bellies with dried beef and pan bread and waited for Shorty to return with his report. Except that Gabe didn't wait. He spread out his bedroll and went to sleep. Out beyond the light of the campfire, Conrad paced in the darkness. He'd had hunches before but never one this strong. Maybe *foreboding* would be a better word for this undercurrent of feeling he couldn't shake.

There was light enough to see by when he heard Shorty's horse returning. The little man rode up and swung down from the saddle.

"What did you learn?" asked Conrad.

"Your hunch was right on target, boss. You ain't going to believe what's happened."

The others gathered around to listen. Even Gabe. It turned out Shorty was right. The story he told was incredible.

"Gillaspy's gone crazy," said Conrad. "Hanging a man without any sign of a trial and for no reason. It's a wonder the townspeople didn't grab that little toad and hang him on the gallows instead."

"I wonder what Pa thought of being throwed into a jail cell," said Gabe. "He ain't used to that kind of treatment."

Conrad noticed that there was no apology from Thurston's middle son. The fact that he'd been right and Gabe had been wrong was forgotten. But not by him. And not by the men who rode with him.

"There may be a hanging yet," said Shorty. "One of 'em shot a guard. That's how they escaped."

Worse and worse, thought Conrad.

"Is there a posse after 'em?" he asked.

"Yep. A posse left at dawn yesterday. They're in big trouble. Gillaspy ain't sheriff no more. The council went and gave the job to that Lockridge fellow you hired. He's going to wear a star until they can hold an election."

Conrad shook his head in dismay at the way things were going. Somehow, he wasn't surprised about Lockridge, though. He'd sensed something about the man from the first, like there was more to him than met the eye. For sure, the new sheriff of Piedmont wasn't cut from ordinary cloth.

"Well," said Gabe, "are you just going to stand here jawing while my pa is in trouble?"

Conrad turned on him. "We'd all be back at the ranch if you'd had your way. Now, you can shut your mouth. I'm giving the orders and I intend to keep on giving them. If you want to get your pa and your brothers out of this alive, you'll do what I say."

"Keep your hand away from that sidearm, Gabe!" Shorty ordered. His own Smith and Wesson was already drawn.

Conrad watched as Gabe raised his hands. It was plain to see the murderous hatred in his eyes. Conrad owed Shorty his life.

"Nobody talks to me like that and gets away with it," said Gabe. "I promise you're both going to rue this day."

Conrad fought down the urge to deck the young fool.

"We'll take this up later after we've got your pa out of this scrape," he said.

"You can count on it."

Conrad turned to Shorty. "Were you able to find out how many were in that posse?"

"Best I could learn there was Lockridge, the Chinese fellow, a stranger, Wade's killer, and a couple of men from the town. I reckon six in all."

"There's six of us," said Gabe, "and Ben and Thad are with Pa. So is Hogue, Birdie, and Gillaspy. Together, we've got 'em outnumbered two to one."

"Not quite," said Shorty. "The way they tell it, Hogue had this burr under his saddle about Lockridge. He started a fight out back of the saloon and Lockridge finished it. When they made the jailbreak, Hogue was still over at the doctor's place. He'd been patched up and put to bed. After the boss and the others were gone, they brung Hogue over and locked him in a cell. He's the only prisoner."

As far as Conrad was concerned, Hogue could stay there until he rotted. But even without him, the numbers looked good. All he and his men had to do was catch up to Thurston and the others. If he could pull his boss' irons out of the fire this time, he might even be in for a share of the ranch. At the very least, the old man would owe him so much that he couldn't fire him.

"All right," he said. "Get ready to ride."

"They say the boss headed east toward the mountains," said Shorty. "Guess he figured it was the best thing for him to do. Here's the bad part. They don't have any spare mounts. The ones I spoke to don't think they took any water or food with 'em, either."

Not entirely bad news. It would mean that Thurston

and his boys would appreciate him even more. He'd been careful to pack plenty of supplies, including food and water. But they had to catch up and deal with the posse.

"Let's go," he said.

He made sure that Gabe was never at his back. Shorty was keeping watch too.

Six riders with spare mounts and a couple of pack mules headed east, taking care to avoid the town. It gave Conrad a measure of satisfaction to think of the arrogant Hogue, bruised and beaten, sitting in the jail behind bars.

Jake climbed down from the saddle and shaded his eyes as he looked into the distance. There was no sign of the outlaws, but they'd left a trail. The tracks of four horses and four sets of boots were clear as day.

"They're spelling their horses," he said. "That'll give us a chance to gain on them."

"They can't stay ahead of us at the rate they're going," said Grady. "Looks like they'd know that."

"I expect they've got someplace in mind. Someplace short of the mountains."

Miguel's expression was grim. "Not the Santos Village," he whispered. It sounded very much like a prayer.

"That would be a dumb thing for them to do," said Jake.

"Desperate men do dumb things," said Schmidt.

Miguel looked stricken and Jake wished the barkeep had kept silent.

Another hour passed before Jake held up his hand, a signal for them to stop.

"There," he pointed. "They've veered off. They're not headed for the village at all."

"Looks more like they're aiming for Gebhardt's place," said Grady.

Now, it was Chung Li's turn to look worried.

"Mr. Gebhardt is a cautious man," he said. "Very little takes him by surprise. When they arrive, I know he will be prepared."

From what Jake had seen of the man, he had to agree. Gebhardt could be a powerful friend or a formidable foe. What's more, Thurston's little band had shot his hired hand, Tidwell. When Gebhardt found out, he wasn't going to be pleased.

Thurston lay belly-down on the ridge-top, observing the area around the big ranch house. Everything looked as it should. He'd decided that under cover of darkness they'd sneak down, steal fresh horses, and slake their thirst. With water, food, and fast mounts, they'd be able to make it to the mountains.

It was because of Gillaspy's foolishness that him and the boys were in all of this trouble. Unless he could figure a way out, he stood to lose everything. He chided himself for ever installing that blundering donkey in the sheriff's office. He promised himself that once they were safe, the first thing he'd do was get rid of him. But safety was a long way off and Gillaspy's gun was sure to be needed.

Gingerly, he crawled away from the ridge and made his way down to where the others were waiting. He noticed that Gillaspy stood apart from his sons. He looked for all the world like a sly old fox trying to decide which chicken to attack first. A wise man doesn't turn his back on a predator.

"What'd you find out, Pa?" said Thad.

"There's not many hands around the place. With all the Indian trouble that we've had, Gebhardt's probably sending more of them out to see to the cattle."

"There's safety in numbers," said Gillaspy. Thurston wondered if he suspected the only reason he was still alive was because they needed him to add to their own number.

"Whatcha going to do, Pa?" said Thad.

"We're going to sneak down there tonight and take what we need."

"Then on to the mountains?" said Gabe.

"Yeah. At least for a while until the town cools off."

"Them people ain't cooling off after what we done," said Gillaspy. "If we don't go back and show 'em who's boss, we're going to lose Piedmont altogether."

Ben gave him a look of contempt.

"You won't have to go back there," he said. "They're coming after you."

From the expression on Gillaspy's face, Ben's reminder hit the mark. He looked downright scared.

"If you want to live through this," said Thurston, "you'd better do like I say."

There appeared to be no more bravado in the exsheriff. It had all disappeared like mist in the sunshine.

As soon as it was dark, they got ready to move. They would have only the lights in the night sky to see by, but Thurston was more than ready.

"Now, follow me and do like you're told," he ordered.

Rather than going over the ridge, they made their way around the south end. A precaution. Even in the moonlight they would have been skylined to the eyes of anyone who happened to look up in that direction.

As they approached, the place was eerily silent. No watchdogs barked a warning. Not that he'd seen any earlier. A mistake on Gebhardt's part. While Ben headed toward the cook shack for food supplies, Thad filled waterskins and canteens. Thurston took the reins of the horses.

He and Gillaspy separated and made their way to the corral. Had it been totally dark, they could still have found it simply by following the pungent smell of horse droppings. They'd almost reached their goal when he heard Gillaspy stumble and mutter a curse. Someone else heard him too.

"What the . . . ?" A man appeared from the shadows and glanced in Gillaspy's direction. He was crouched and the man failed to spot him in the darkness. Thurston backed up against a corral pole and held his breath. The man walked forward, searching for the source of the noise. When he was only a few feet away from where Thurston was hiding, he paused to listen. Thurston drew his .44 and smashed the butt of it into his head. Gebhardt's man fell to the ground with a soft thud.

Gillaspy sprinted the short distance to the corral. There, he put his foot on one of the bars and swung himself over. Thurston waited outside, watching. The house was still quiet and dark.

Gillaspy picked out four mounts and put bridles on

them. Then he eased them through the gate and fastened it back.

"Gotta hurry and get the saddles switched," he whispered.

Thurston helped and they were soon ready to ride.

Across the yard, a shadow emerged from the cook shack. Ben hurried toward them carrying two large burlap sacks. It looked like he'd struck pay dirt. Thad was next with the water bags and canteens.

They divided the load. The guard was still out and no alarm had been raised. Luck was with them. Quietly, they led the fresh mounts away, leaving behind the worn out horses they'd stolen at Piedmont. When they'd put some distance between themselves and the hacienda they mounted up and rode off.

Ahead of them, the dark outline of the mountains was visible in the moonlight. For Thurston, the high country represented a haven, a place from which to fight back.

"Soon," he said to the night wind. "Soon we'll be in the mountains where we can defeat our enemies."

Chapter Fourteen

Klaus Gebhardt had just finished shaving when a knock sounded on his bedroom door.

"What is it?" he called, struggling with the top button on his shirt.

His houseman, Karl, entered. "Herr Gebhardt, McCoy just brought word that thieves sneaked in here last night and stole some of the horses. One of them took food from the cook house too."

"How could this be? What about the guard that was posted?"

"McCoy reported that he was found unconscious."

Not waiting for the rest of the story from Karl, he rushed out to where McCoy was waiting. Together they joined the others. The men had gathered around Seth Hyatt, who was now awake, but gray-faced and bruised with a knot on his head.

"It weren't Injuns who done this," said Hyatt. "Look at them boot prints."

He concurred. Not only because of the prints and the shod horses that had been left behind, but had Apaches managed to slip in, they would have burned the place and left them all dead. He would double the guard.

"Do you suppose it was that bunch from over by Piedmont?" said McCoy.

He suspected it was. For sure, it wouldn't have been Lockridge or the men who rode with him. Lockridge stacked up as being a man of honor. He'd have come in and asked for whatever he needed and he wouldn't have attacked Hyatt that way. Still, he was puzzled. If the thieves were Gillaspy or the Thurstons, what could have brought them out here, desperate for horses and food?

It wasn't long before he got his answer.

"Riders!" shouted one of his men, pointing toward the west.

He looked up to see six horsemen coming off the ridge. Whoever they were, they weren't sneaking in as the others had done. When they got closer, he was able to recognize Lockridge and Chung Li.

"It'll be all right," he told his men, whose weapons were drawn. "I expect they're after our nighttime visitors."

Jake could tell from the looks of things that there had been trouble. Gebhardt and several of his hands were gathered around an injured man. He and the others rode in slowly. He noted the suspicious looks they were given as they reined up at the corral. He was glad Chung Li was with them.

"Well, well," said Gebhardt, eyeing the badge on Jake's vest. "I see you've taken on a new job."

"Sorry to say I have, but it's not to my liking. Gillaspy tried to hang Russ Walkenshaw—no trial, no reason. It would have been straight out murder. He was trying to show the town that he was running it. Then Thurston and his boys threw in with him. We couldn't let Walkenshaw hang so we put them all in jail."

Gebhardt eyed him thoughtfully. "That explains a few things. It appears they didn't like their new quarters. Otherwise, you wouldn't be here this fine morning, and I wouldn't be missing four of my best horses and a good many food supplies."

"I figured they might be headed for your place. They left town in too big a hurry to take any water or food. Only guns. And they had one horse apiece. I didn't expect, with just the four of them, that they'd be foolish enough to stop at Santos' village. Santos and his people are on the alert for them."

Gebhardt nodded. "That's a tough old man and he's got the guns to back him up. I think Gillaspy and Thurston have taken a page from your book, Lockridge. They're headed for the mountains."

That much was clear. Now, he had to break the bad news. He glanced over at Chung Li who took the hint.

"Mr. Gebhardt," said Chung Li. "I'm sorry to have to tell you this. Tidwell is dead. They shot him last night when they escaped."

Gebhardt's facial muscles tightened but he took the news stoically.

"Tidwell was a good man."

"Too good to die the way he did," said Jake.

"Saddle my horse!" Gebhardt yelled to one of his men.

"Are you joining us?" asked Jake.

"Of course. Tidwell worked for me. I'll see to it that his killers hang."

A short time later, they were on the trail again.

"The horses they left behind were pretty well used up," said Gebhardt. "But the ones they took should get them into the mountains without any trouble."

"I figured as much," said Jake. "Once we get to the high country, we need to be on the lookout for an ambush."

Something else concerned him too. When Thurston and his boys failed to return to his ranch, Conrad would be sure to form a search party. Not only did they have to be wary of an ambush, they had to watch their back trail, as well.

Beyond the ranch, the terrain was broken and uneven. It was made up of low rolling foothills and washes, valleys and rises. Largely because of this, they weren't able to catch sight of the gang they were hunting. But from the sign that was left behind, Jake could tell he was gaining on them.

Darkness found them on higher ground, camped among scrubby piñons. With the horses securely tethered, they built a small fire in a pit to hide its light from both outlaws and Apaches. When it was time to bed down, they took turns keeping watch. Jake volunteered to be first. In the silence of the windswept night, he felt a strong sense of loneliness. As with most nights since he'd been away from home, he thought of Alicia.

If I ever get back to you, my wife, I don't intend to leave again. Not for anything. Not even for a prodigal brother-in-law.

The sun was still below the horizon when they broke camp and mounted up. It wasn't long before they'd left the cedars and piñons behind and were wending their way through a ponderosa forest. The air was thinner this high on the mountain. It was fresh and light and scented with pine. Single file, they followed an old trail, the same one the outlaws had taken. One of them must have known about it. Hours passed as the sun rose higher.

Suddenly they came to the edge of a clearing. Jake signaled them to stop. If they entered, they'd be exposing themselves in that wide open space. It was the perfect setup for an ambush. He tried to see into the forest beyond. Nothing was stirring. Still, all of his instincts were warning him of danger.

"What is it?" said Decker, who'd ridden up beside him.

"I don't like this. I feel like a fly about to step into a spider's web."

"I don't see anything."

"Neither do I. It's just a gut feeling."

"I believe you have good instincts, Lockridge," said Gebhardt. "Hunches have saved many lives and they've made gamblers rich."

"We'll skirt the clearing," said Jake.

But before he could move, there was a gunshot. A bullet slammed into a nearby tree trunk not a foot from Jake's head. Instinctively, he threw himself off the horse and hit the ground rolling. Enemy guns started blazing. He crawled into the underbrush and fanned three shots in their direction. Decker and the others were firing too. All around him, the pine-scented air was tainted with the odor of sulfur.

Before the smoke obscured everything, Jake noted that the Thurstons' position across the clearing was on higher ground. Through a screen of trees, he'd spotted a rock spill—a granite fortress. The enemy had chosen well.

Long ago his father had given him a piece of advice. "In order to defeat the enemy, son, you need to secure the high ground."

Too late, Pa. It's already taken.

When a sharp gust of wind blew away most of the smoke, Jake caught a glimpse of maroon plaid cloth. It looked to be part of a man's shirt. He aimed and fired. The shot was followed by a loud yelp, and the cloth disappeared.

During a sudden lull, Jake called out. "Give yourself up, Gillaspy! You'll be given a fair trial, unlike Sandoval and Deputy Walkenshaw."

Left unsaid were the words "before they hang you." But then, they weren't needed. Gillaspy was aware that someone would hang for Tidwell's murder. Gillaspy's reply was a bullet. It plowed into the dirt a few inches in front of where Jake was crouched. Again, the peace of the forest was destroyed by a volley of gunfire. Jake heard a moan nearby to his left. Someone had been hit.

A couple of minutes later Decker crawled up beside him. "Schmidt's been shot and he's losing a lot of blood. We've got to get him away from here and take care of him."

The outlaws had created a standoff. They were holed up behind a fortress of rocks with plenty of water and supplies. If he and his men tried to rush them, they'd be cut down before they got halfway across the clearing.

"All right," he agreed. "Let's pull back."

They retreated into the deep woods. He helped Gebhardt and Decker retrieve the horses that had scattered when the firing started. Schmidt was half dragged, half carried by Grady and Miguel. Jake took one look at the wounded man and knew he couldn't go much farther, even on horseback.

"Remember that rock shelf we passed on the way," he said, "the one that opens out into a ledge. We'll stop there for a time."

"What about Gillaspy and his bunch?" said Decker. "Won't they come after us?"

How quickly hunters could become the quarry.

"No," he said. "At least I don't think they're crazy enough to do that. There's too many of us. Besides they have the perfect place to hole up and wait for reinforcements."

"Reinforcements?"

"When Thurston and his sons fail to show up at their ranch, Conrad will no doubt investigate to see what happened to them. Then he'll be on their trail. On our trail. And he'll have a lot of men with him."

Gebhardt nodded in agreement. It was clear he'd been thinking along the same lines.

They made their way down to the rock shelf where they deposited Schmidt on a blanket. He breathed a sigh and closed his eyes. Blood had drenched his shirt on one side. Grady fetched a bottle of alcohol from a saddlebag and poured it liberally on the wound. Then he stanched the flow of blood with a bandanna.

"Is the bullet still in there?" Jake asked.

"I don't think so. It appears to have passed on through. What it hit on the way, I'm not sure. If he's lucky it wasn't anything vital."

Jake liked the barkeep. Admired his backbone. Hoped he was lucky.

Conrad studied the Gebhardt ranch from his vantage point. Smoke drifted upward from the cookhouse smoke-pipe where it was sent scudding southward by the wind. The corral was filled with horses. From what he could see, they were fine ones. Over at the forge, an old man was busy shaping a horseshoe.

"See anything?" asked Gabe who'd come up behind him, something Conrad could ill afford to let happen.

"Everything looks normal. But your pa and the others would be in bad need of fresh mounts and they'd be in want of water and provisions. This is the one place they could get them."

"What about the other tracks?"

"The posse? They weren't far behind."

"You think Pa and my brothers sneaked in there, grabbed what they needed, and got away?"

"My guess is they did."

A look of relief flitted across the middle son's face.

"Then we'd better give that ranch a wide berth and pick up their trail on the other side."

Conrad fought back the urge to deck him. Gabe, who'd been against this rescue all along, was now vying for control.

"I've already decided to do that," he said coldly. "But before we find your pa and your brothers, we'll run into that posse."

Gabe smirked. "I'm counting on it, old man. If we can trap 'em between us and Pa, we'll cut 'em to ribbons."

Conrad leaned back in his saddle, weary from the long ride and all that had been going on before. "I'm way ahead of you, boy," he said. "That's exactly what I had in mind."

Gabe glared at him. "Then we'd best stop sitting here jawin', old man. Let's get on down to the others and get a move on."

With that last thrust, Gabe Thurston wheeled his horse and rode off.

Conrad allowed himself another moment of rest and silence, a brief time in which to collect himself. Then he followed after Gabe.

Conrad and his men made a wide sweep, bypassing the ranch house. When they were well beyond it, they turned back toward the south where they picked up the trail again. There wasn't any doubt that Thurston and his boys were headed for the high country. No surprise. In their place, he'd have done the same thing. The sign was clear. The outfit from Piedmont was hot on their trail.

He regretted that Hogue wasn't on the run with his boss. The fool was dumb enough to get himself shot and that would please Conrad just fine. He was getting too old for all this aggravation, and Hogue was one of the aggravations he could do without.

He thought about Gebhardt and his ranch hands. Had someone back there spotted him and his outfit? He'd only seen one old man and he'd been busy at his work. A fifty-fifty chance, he decided. But if the alarm had been sounded, what would the German do? Would he follow? No doubt, the posse had told him of Tidwell's murder and everyone knew that Tidwell had worked for Gebhardt. They also knew that Gebhardt had a reputation for arrogance and for having a bad temper when riled. He was the kind who'd want revenge, even for a thirty-a-month cowhand, if that cowhand worked for him. Another reason for Conrad to watch his back.

Schmidt was racked with chills. There was no help for it, Jake had to build a fire. He kept it small and contained within a circle of stones. The pines that surrounded the stone shelf would filter the smoke and render it invisible to those above. Not that he thought they would move out and attack. Grady made hot tea and got Schmidt to drink a little of it.

"Nothing better for shock," said the hotel owner. "I always keep some with me."

Jake made coffee for the rest of them and passed around jerky and canned peaches. Then he leaned against a tree and waited for the cover of darkness.

Still within shouting distance of the outlaws, they

heard an Indian war whoop while Miguel was pouring coffee. He froze, coffee pot in hand, cup half filled.

Gillaspy hollered, "We know you're down there! Come on up 'cause we got something for you!"

"They're taunting us," said Gebhardt. "Trying to lure us into range. Into a trap."

"Ignore them," said Jake. "They're staying put. Until their water runs out, anyway."

Gebhardt leaned back against his grounded saddle and looked thoughtful.

"It seems to me that the next time we go after them we should divide our forces," he said. "Half to engage in a frontal assault while the other half slips around and attacks from the rear."

"Good plan," Jake agreed. "But consider the men we're after. Gillaspy acts like he's a bubble off plumb. Not much that he does makes any sense. Then there's Thad Thurston who isn't too bright. Old man Thurston isn't afraid of anything, but he's so full of himself that he's a poor tactician. The way I see it, the dangerous one is Ben. He's canny and he has a mean streak."

"And what do you think Ben will do?"

"I have a hunch that he'll anticipate us. When we attack, he'll have the others prepared."

Decker, Miguel, and Chung Li were listening with interest.

"I'll grant you Ben's the smartest one of the bunch," said Decker, "but will his old man pay any attention to him?"

"That's the question," said Jake. "Thurston is used to

calling the shots, but he's up against it now. My guess is he will."

"Then my plan isn't apt to work," said Gebhardt.

"Likely not. But there's more. I've got a feeling that Conrad is following. And he won't come alone. With him on one side of us and Thurston's outfit on the other, we'd be trapped. I'm afraid it's a question, now, of survival."

Chapter Fifteen

Jake was certain that trouble was coming. The shelf they were camped on became a ledge and they dared not be caught on it. They had to move.

"How is Schmidt doing?" he asked.

"The bleeding has stopped," said Grady. "But he's still having chills."

"Can he be moved?"

"If necessary, I suppose. But I wouldn't try to take him very far."

The others looked at Jake expectantly.

"Stay here and keep alert," he said. "I'm going to scout around. This isn't a good place to be if we're attacked."

"How much time do you think you have?" asked Decker.

"No telling. Not much, if my guess is right. I doubt if Conrad is a patient man."

He checked his pistol and made sure that his knife was in place. Then he grabbed the Winchester and mounted the bay.

"I'll be back as soon as I can," he promised.

Away from the shelf, the forest was dense. Silently, he threaded his way among the pines. Here and there, he notched one in an inconspicious place, marking his path. A north wind rippled the needles, playing the gentle music that had sounded since the beginning of time. That same north wind caused him to shiver and shrug deeper into his coat. He pulled his hat low. In the shade of the forest, the light was beginning to wane and he knew the dangers of groping his way in the wilderness at night.

If somehow he could find a place like the one where Thurston and his bunch were holed up, they'd stand a chance. He was angry at himself for acting without considering all the factors. As the newly appointed sheriff, it had been his job to form a posse and go after the killers, but he should have given more thought to Conrad. All he could think of at the time was running Gillaspy and the Thurstons to ground. Keep them from doing more harm to others. But now, the tables were turned. All the enemy had to do was play a waiting game. Fend off the posse and wait for reinforcements.

He worried about the men he'd left on that exposed shelf of land. Cornered, there was no place to go except into the face of the outlaws or over the side of the mountain. What's more, if Conrad had begun to worry sooner than later, he'd only be a short distance behind.

There was barely enough light to see by when he found what he was searching for. He'd figured that if boulders had washed out and fallen from the heights back where the outlaws were holed up, then others were likely to have tumbled, as well. What he'd come upon were three of varying sizes. These boulders were large enough to provide concealment and protection to the entire posse. Directly behind them lay a steep slope. It was the route down which those granite giants had slid millennia before. It was like a wall, for the angle was too sharp for horses to either climb or descend, at least not easily. Now, he needed to get back to the others and lead them here. But he'd taken too long and it was too dark. Stumbling around in the black of night wouldn't do. Anyone who tried it would become hopelessly lost. There was no choice. He had to bed down and wait for dawn. He only hoped that Conrad was of the same mind.

Rolled in his blankets on the side of the mountain, he tried to sleep. But sleep was elusive. Troublesome thoughts crept in uninvited. Someone connected to the Thurstons had shot Wade. It had to have been one of them. Hundreds of dollars had come up missing, then Hogue was suddenly flush with money. Maybe Hogue had killed him, but Wade was a good shot and Hogue was a cautious man. He was the kind who'd attack only when he had a strong advantage. Had he witnessed the shooting and been paid off by the killer? Or had he found where the money was stashed? Why had Ben lied and said he'd seen Miguel do the shooting? Was Ben the killer? Was he only protecting the killer? A third alternative came to mind. Maybe Ben jumped to the conclusion that Miguel had shot his brother. Then, realizing the lack of evidence, he'd lied to ensure his conviction and keep public opinion on the side of the Thurstons. Ben was the kind who'd never be bothered by conscience.

Jake tried thinking about the problem in a different way. Who could he mark off the list of suspects? Besides Miguel and possibly old man Thruston, he couldn't think of anyone. Besides Wade's brothers, the killer could have been Conrad, or Birdie, or Shorty, or any of them. Any one of them could have had a motive. Even Gillaspy. He might have had a falling out with the heir apparent and plugged him. The killer would have needed to hide the money. The fact that Hogue was flaunting it made Jake think he was innocent, at least of the killing. He may simply have come across it and claimed it for himself. Jake had a lot of questions and no answers. He was determined to stay alive and find them.

As soon as he could see his hand in front of his face, Jake rolled up his blankets and started back to the others. There had been no sound of gunfire, which would have echoed across the mountain. There was still time. The notches he'd made on the trees guided him through the wilderness until he got back to camp.

Gebhardt was standing guard when he rode up. Hot coffee was waiting.

"Have you heard anything from Gillaspy and the rest of 'em?" Jake asked.

"No," said Decker as he poured Jake a cup of coffee. "They're just sitting up there waiting for something to happen."

"We've seen nothing of that outfit from Thurston's ranch, either," said Grady. "What's more, I hope we don't."

So did Jake, but he wasn't counting on it. From what he'd heard about Gabe, the middle son, there would have been nothing to worry about. Gabe never did more than he absolutely had to. But Conrad was a thinking man and he rode for the brand. Conrad would be on his way.

"We've got to pack the gear and move out," he said.

Schmidt was looking a little better. His color had returned and he'd been able to eat some soup made with jerky.

"Don't worry about me," said the barkeep. "Put me on a horse and I won't be any trouble at all."

Grady and Gebhardt helped the wounded man to mount. Then they all followed Jake as he led them to the refuge.

"They'll track us, you know," said Gebhardt.

"I'm counting on it," Jake replied. "Let's face it. We're not fighting for ourselves alone, but for all the people in Piedmont. Even for those who live in the area, people like the ones in Santos' village. Thurston intends to run this part of Arizona like his own little barony, and Gillaspy wants a share of the power. They won't stop unless we stop them."

"You're quite right," said Gebhardt. "We're all that

stands in their way. They can't afford to let us off this mountain alive."

They'd not yet reached their destination when they heard two gunshots in quick succession. A signal. They paused to listen. Two answering shots followed.

"I believe that Conrad has arrived," said Jake.

They hurried on, wending their way through the pines until they came, at last, to the boulders. Behind their fortress-like expanse, Jake and the others ground-staked the horses. Then they took positions facing the newly broken trail. All except Schmidt who'd been eased off his mount and placed gently onto a blanket. He lay there quietly, his strength expended.

"Jake, I'm worried," said Decker. "No telling how many of them will be coming after us. What if they flank us?"

"It's likely they'll try. That's why I'm leaving you and taking off on foot. I'm going to work my way over to a place where I'll be behind them when they attack. They might think they're surrounded. Maybe that will worry 'em a little."

"Good idea," said Decker. "I'll go with you."

"No, amigo," Miguel protested. "You're needed here."

"He's right," said Jake. "With Schmidt wounded they'll need your gun."

"All right," he said, though he clearly didn't like following the order.

Jake left them and made his way to a place across from the boulders. There he settled down to wait. He didn't have to wait long. He heard the enemy approaching before he actually saw them. They'd joined forces. The old bull of the herd led the way, followed by Ben and the foreman. Thad was slumped in the saddle, a makeshift bandage on his arm. Evidently he'd been the one to take Jake's bullet. Gillaspy was relegated to the back. Ten in all was Jake's count.

Gebhardt, who'd been left in command, opened the ball. The outlaws lunged for cover and returned fire. They had the advantage in numbers, but this time Jake's posse had the higher ground.

Thurston's outfit divided, as Jake had expected, and began a flanking movement. Jake dropped to one knee and squeezed off a shot. One of the outlaws fell, one that Jake couldn't name. The smoke was thick, making it hard to see. A volley of gunfire was aimed in his direction. The smokescreen was now working to his advantage. Jake crawled through the underbrush to the cover of a ponderosa.

Conrad wasn't surprised when he heard the shot. He'd been expecting an ambush. He castigated himself for coming to Thurston's rescue. No sooner was the rancher found cowering behind those rocks than he up and took over command.

The order was given to divide and storm the fortress. Conrad felt sick inside. Chances were he was going to die in the wilderness for a man he'd come to despise. He nodded that he understood and began to crawl in the direction Thurston had indicated. The smell of death was all around him. First one, then another of his men fell. Thurston was nowhere to be seen.

Under the cover of smoke and scrub, Conrad crawled off to the side into deep cover. Let Thurston storm his own fortresses.

Jake had stirred up a hornet's nest. A couple of them had him pinned down and were pouring it on. He stopped firing to reload. His rifle lay beside him.

"Come on! Let's get him!" came a shout. "He's out of ammunition."

A man in a brown flannel shirt rose up from the brush and sprinted toward the place where Jake was pinned. Jake picked up the rifle and fired. Brown Flannel went down. The other fellow who'd started after him, fell back. Jake crawled deeper into cover. Squinting through the smoke, he caught sight of Thurston. He was leading the attack, but was too close to the boulders for them to get a shot at him from the other side. It was up to Jake to stop him. He ran forward, gun drawn.

"Thurston!" he yelled. "Over here!"

The big man turned. But before Jake could fire, he felt a hard blow to his side. He'd been shot. Not by Thurston, though. He looked over and saw the hate-twisted face of Ben.

The pistol in Jake's hand grew heavy, too heavy to lift and fire. Ben's shape began to waver like a ghostly specter. Then there was nothing.

It was fully dark when he opened his eyes. He was

cold. Colder than he'd ever been in his life. His mouth was dry and he wanted a drink. His side hurt too. When he put his hand underneath his vest to feel if he was wounded, his fingers came away covered in blood. He struggled to sit up. Slowly his memory returned, along with a sense of alarm. *What's happened to the others?* Pulling the bandanna from around his neck, he packed it against the wound to stanch the bleeding. Then he got to his knees, and using a young pine to steady himself, stood upright. A quick check told him his pistol was gone. But the knife was still in his belt and his fallen body had shielded the rifle.

"A horse," he mumbled to himself. "I need a horse."

He half walked, half stumbled to where they'd been picketed. They were gone. So were his friends and allies. He'd been abandoned and left for dead. Thurston and Gillaspy had won, for what could a dead man do? He slid to a sitting position and leaned against a boulder. He touched something fuzzy. It was Schmidt's blanket. Covering himself with it, he slept.

When he awoke, it was early morning. He was no longer bleeding. Still, there was danger of putrefaction. He needed alcohol, whiskey, or even clean, clear water to cleanse the wound. None were to be had.

What had happened to his brother-in-law, his friend, and the others who'd joined them? There were no bodies. No graves, either. That left another possibility. Hostages. Knowing Gillaspy's lust for power and Thurston's pride and hunger for vengeance, they may have taken them back to Piedmont for a public execution. Jake leaned back against the boulder and closed his eyes. He was high on a mountain and the nearest place he could get help was Gebhardt's ranch, which was many miles away. He was wounded. He'd lost a lot of blood and was on foot. Unless he could suddenly grow wings, there was nothing in the world he could do to save the men who'd risked their lives to join him.

Chapter Sixteen

Jake struggled to his feet. Still draped in the blanket, he took a tentative step, then another. He licked his dry, cracked lips. There was no water to be had. After a few yards, a sudden wave of dizziness threatened to topple him. He managed to stay upright and keep moving.

The realization that he was powerless caused him anger and anguish that was worse than the pain of his wound. He was fearful for those who'd been captured and were sure to be killed. Somehow he would survive, he vowed. When he got off the mountain, he would hunt down the killers one by one.

Armed with the rifle, he painfully retraced his route along the pine-notched trail. Twice he stumbled and fell. Twice he got up and trudged on. Hours must have passed before he reached the ledge where they'd first withdrawn to care for Schmidt. He was making his way across it when a rider appeared from the stand of pines that ridged the edge. To Jake's surprise, it was Thurston's foreman, Conrad. He rode forward, leading a saddled horse. His gun was holstered. What was he up to?

"Stop right there!" Jake ordered, bringing up the rifle.

"Put that down," said Conrad. "You'd best not shoot the man who's about to save your hide."

"What do you mean by that?"

"Just what I said. I've had more than enough of Matt Thurston and his boys, and I don't cotton to that dumb Gillaspy, neither."

"Why are you here? What happened to my posse?"

"It's about time you started worrying about 'em. They're prisoners on their way to Piedmont. Thurston has it in mind to hang 'em. Personally, I don't think the barkeep is going to make it all the way to town. He was bad hurt. Moving him like they're doing isn't good."

Jake fought the impulse to shoot this man who'd been one of them. Conrad sensed his conflict and shook his head. "Don't. You shoot me and you haven't a prayer of saving any of your men. I'm their only chance."

"What have you got in mind?" Jake asked warily.

"First off, I'm going to fix up that wound of yours and give you some water and food. Then you're going to climb on that horse over yonder and we're heading for Gebhardt's ranch as fast as we can go. I figure his boys will be more'n glad to save their boss from a public hanging."

"Then let's get on with it."

Jake took a swig of water from the canteen that

Conrad handed him. Then Conrad examined Jake's wound. "Looks like the bullet passed on through. At least I won't have to dig for lead. Good thing. That's something I never cared to do."

Next, he took a bottle of whiskey from one of his saddlebags and poured it liberally into the wound. Jake gasped.

"It's worth the sting," said Conrad. "That whiskey will probably save your life."

After he'd applied a bandage, he handed Jake a piece of jerky and a hard biscuit. Then they got ready to ride.

"That horse belonged to one of my boys," said Conrad, indicating the roan that Jake was astride. "He won't be needing it anymore."

They made their way down the mountainside, moving as fast as they dared. The pines gave way to cedars.

"Try to stay in the saddle, Lockridge," said Conrad, breaking the silence that had settled between them. "We've got to get to Gebhardt's ranch and there's no time to waste."

It was well after dark by the time they arrived. Jake called out to whoever was guarding the place.

"Come on in," was the reply, "but remember you're covered."

Jake quickly told his story. It didn't take Gebhardt's men long to get ready to ride. He and Conrad were given fresh horses and someone loaned him a coat to replace the blanket. As they headed out into the night, moonlight bathed the desert landscape. There were fifteen of them—enough to challenge Thurston if only they could make it in time. Along with the coat, Jake had borrowed a pistol, a well-used Smith and Wesson .44. He was prepared.

To their advantage, they wouldn't be expected. The outlaws had bypassed the ranch and had left him for dead. They'd left Conrad for dead too. Another thing in their favor was the fact that both Gillaspy and Thurston were show-offs. They'd want a public hanging with all the townspeople present. For best effect, they'd likely stage it early in the day, after everyone had been notified the day before. This meant that Jake and his allies would have another day and night.

When they stopped to let the horses blow, Jake had a word with Conrad.

"We can't all go riding into town like this," he said. "They've got the prisoners for hostages and they're apt to start shooting them until we back off."

"Seems to me it's a risk we have to take."

"What if I slip into town ahead of you. Maybe I can protect them when the shooting starts."

"You're welcome to try, but you don't look like you're in all that good a shape to me."

Jake couldn't deny the pain in his side where the bullet had entered and exited. Still, he hadn't lost consciousness and he'd lost very little blood after Conrad had bandaged it.

"I'll be fine," he said.

"Then we'll pull up behind that rise near town and wait. You can ride on in before it gets daylight and see what you can do."

They continued the following day and stopped for the night at the foot of the rise. Jake got a few hours' sleep before he left them to go on alone.

Stars were still visible when he rode the borrowed horse through the outskirts of town. Up ahead, looking surreal in shadow and moonlight, a scaffolding rose in front of the jail, a duplicate of its predecessor. No doubt, forced labor had hastened its construction. Neither Thurston nor Gillaspy was apt to forget the pleasure the townspeople had taken in burning the first one.

Jake turned down a side street and entered a narrow alley. He was headed toward the back of the livery stable when a shadowy figure stepped out to block his way. There was enough light to see that it was Hogue. He'd been released from jail and he held a pistol in his hand.

"I've been waiting for you, Lockridge. I didn't think for one minute you was dead like they claimed. Now, I've got my chance."

Jake froze. A gunshot would alert Gillaspy and the others.

"You started it, Hogue," he said, hoping to keep him talking until he could think of something to do.

"I'm going to finish it too. Get down off that horse."

Jake's hand was close to the grips of his .44, but he dared not use it.

"Come on! Quit stalling!"

Keeping his gun side away from Hogue, he slid out of the saddle.

"Now, put your hands in the air so I can see 'em."

It was now—or maybe never. Still, Jake chose to wait

rather than sound the alarm. Hogue relieved him of his borrowed gun.

"Now, walk down to the other end of the alley and don't try nothing funny. We're going inside the livery barn where the shot won't be so loud. You think about it all the way. Think about how Hogue don't let nobody get the better of him."

With his left hand, the outlaw grabbed the reins of Jake's horse and followed close behind. There seemed to be no escape. Already he figured he'd made a mistake not taking that one chance at a shot.

They were passing the back door of the mercantile when Jake heard the sound of a thud behind him. It was followed by a moan. Then a heavy body hit the ground. He turned to find Hogue sprawled in the dirt. A figure stepped out of the shadows. In the dimness, he recognized Birdie.

"Looked like you could use some help," he said. "I never could abide that bully."

"Thanks. I owe you yet again."

"Let's get him tied up and stored under some straw before one of my uncle's men happens along."

Jake retrieved his weapon and took Hogue's. Then, together they dragged the unconscious outlaw to the livery barn. There, Birdie found some piggin' strings and bound Hogue's wrists and ankles. Jake made a gag of his bandanna and they dragged him behind a pile of straw.

"You realize you've picked your side and there's no going back," said Jake.

"I picked it a long time ago," said Birdie. "You see, I'm the one who shot Wade."

Jake was startled by the confession. What had prompted this nervous, frightened young man to kill?

"How did it happen?"

"I was out with Ben and Thad, looking for strays. I managed to drift away on my own without them noticing. I realized this was a chance to escape, so as soon as they were out of sight, I headed south. I was doing all right, too, until Wade spotted me. He was coming back from selling the cattle. I learned later that the two fellows who'd accompanied him had gone on a drunk and Wade left 'em behind. Anyway, he yelled when he saw me. I tried to get away but he cut me off. 'I've got you, now, you little whelp,' he said. 'I'm going to beat you to a pulp. Then I'm going to take you back to Pa and the boys and let them have at you. Teach you to run off.' I didn't even think about it. I grabbed my gun and shot him. Then I rode back to the ranch so they wouldn't suspect that I was the killer."

"Sounds like a clear case of self-defense to me. No jury would convict you of murder."

"Anywhere else, maybe. But here I wouldn't even have got to trial. If I had, it would have been as much of a farce as the trial they had for Sandoval. That's the one thing I regret, what they've done to Sandoval and to the others."

"We'll have to do something about that, Birdie. Are you with me?"

"You bet."

"By the way, was it Hogue that stole the money?"

"I think so. He must have got there right after I left. Probably came looking for me. He knew that Wade would have money in his saddlebags. Then Ben came along looking for me and found Wade. He got all hot to blame somebody and Sandoval was the first man he saw. Lying about it wouldn't have bothered him a bit."

"Looks like they'd have been suspicious with Hogue going around spending money like there was no tomorrow."

"The way he told it was he'd won a lot of money a couple of years back on a horse race. Said he'd stashed it away, waiting 'til he needed it or had the urge to spend it."

"And Thurston and his boys believed that."

"Why not? They'd convinced themselves that Sandoval was the murderer and so he had to be the thief, as well. That was the only motive he could have had for shooting Wade."

It made sense, in a way. But the killing had served as an excuse to take over a town and its government. Thurston was the kind who needed to control people and to run things. Gillaspy was greedy for money and power. Both of them craved people's respect, or rather their fear.

"By the way, Gillaspy is wearing a badge again," said Birdie.

"On whose authority?"

"On Uncle Matt's say-so. Uncle Matt has jailed the judge and appointed himself to every public office except sheriff."

Jake felt a knot of dread in his stomach. The man was insane. But Piedmont was isolated from the rest of the Territory. It was likely there would never be an investigation. Unless something was done, Thurston and Gillaspy would get away with a lot of murders and they'd own the town. At least Thurston would.

"Conrad has joined us," he said.

"I'm not surprised. He may not be the most law-abiding man, but he's got a lot of common sense, and there's a limit to what he'll do."

"He's with a bunch of Gebhardt's men. They'll be riding into town come daylight. But what we've got to do is ensure that Thurston and his flunkies don't kill the prisoners, or use them as hostages, when the attack comes."

"I see. They sure enough give him the upper hand. But what can we do?"

"We need to arm the prisoners."

"How? And with what?"

"Maybe we can get some help on that. Do you know where Maybelle Walkenshaw lives?"

"I think so."

"Well, I'm going out there to see if she has some of her father's weapons. You stay here and guard Hogue until I get back."

Avoiding the main street, he rode out to the house on the edge of town. He tied the reins to the fence and climbed over. The place was dark as he slipped up and tapped on the window. A minute passed before it was slid open.

"Who's out there?" came a woman's voice.

"It's Jake Lockridge. I need to talk to you, but no lights."

She shut the window and opened the back door.

Briefly, he told her what he had in mind to do. "Do you have any weapons?"

"Yes, but not many. My father is a prisoner, too, and I've been worried sick. There's a pistol that Gillaspy didn't confiscate, and a derringer that I carry in my reticule."

"Load them. I need them both."

He was left standing in the doorway while she hurried to comply.

"What else can I do?" she asked when she returned with the weapons.

"Stay here out of sight. I can't predict how things will go."

Back at the livery barn, he handed the guns over to Birdie, along with Hogue's .44.

"I'll never be able to get past the guards, but maybe you can," said Jake. "They think you're one of them. See if you can smuggle these in. If you can, let Decker and the others know that we're coming for them."

Birdie hid the guns under his coat. "I'll try. Wish me luck."

Jake's next stop was the hotel. He entered through the back way and spotted the desk clerk asleep on a cot. There was a candle burning low on a candle stand. Jake eased the keys from their slot above the desk and made his way up the stairs. He let himself into the first room. The occupant was asleep. In the moonlight that spilled through the window, he recognized Gabe's face. Gun drawn, he softly called his name.

Gabe woke with a start.

"Don't make a sound," Jake ordered. "If you do it will be your last."

Beads of sweat glistened on the man's face.

With deft movements Jake bound and gagged him. The whole process was repeated in the next room with Thad. Counting Hogue, that was three less to make trouble. But he was running out of time. Darkness was fading to a dirty gray. He went back to the barn to see if Birdie had returned. He wasn't there. Before the cover of darkness was completely lost, Jake climbed to the roof of the building across from the jail. Here, with rifle in hand, he waited. This was the same place where Tidwell had concealed himself that day.

He tried to spot Birdie, but he was nowhere in sight. Minutes passed and sun streaks started to brighten the eastern sky. Birdie had confirmed that the hangings were scheduled for shortly after dawn. The crowd would soon be gathering. But as the minutes passed, there was no crowd.

Ben stepped out of the jail and looked up and down the street before going back inside. When the door opened again, Gillaspy appeared. Then the prisoners were marched out, their hands tied behind their backs. Thurston and his son followed. Then Birdie. Last was one of the hands from Thruston's ranch. Birdie had failed.

What's more Conrad and the men from Gebhardt's ranch were nowhere to be seen. It was going to be up to Jake.

"Where is everybody?" demanded Gillaspy in a booming voice. "I wanted everybody to watch this and learn."

"I expect they're tired of your grandstanding," said Gebhardt. "It gets a little old after a while."

"Shut up!" said Gillaspy. "You can't hang soon enough to suit me."

"Gebhardt, you can go first," said Thurston, anxious for payback. "Then Sandoval and the others. Now, let's get on with it."

"But there ain't nobody here to watch," said Gillaspy. "Wait until I can get them rousted out."

"Never mind!" yelled Thurston. "I don't care whether they're here or not."

"Up the steps, then," said Gillaspy, putting his gun to Gebhardt's back.

Jake took careful aim at Thurston. If he dropped the herd bull, maybe the others would back off. Still, he couldn't bring himself to do it without a warning.

"Hold it right there, Gillaspy!" he shouted. "I've got a rifle aimed at Thurston.

They all looked up. Ben grabbed for his pistol. Jake swung the rifle just enough and squeezed off a shot. Ben dropped. The prisoners ducked out of the way as the outlaws began firing. Jake crawled to the side of the building and jumped across the narrow gap to land on the roof next door. The impact sent a jarring pain through his wounded side.

Suddenly the shooting stopped. Jake glanced over the rooftop to see what had caused the lull. Gebhardt had gotten his hands loose and was holding a pistol to Thurston's head. Decker had a gun on Gillaspy. Miguel held the derringer. Birdie had stepped back and was covering the remaining outlaws. He'd come through, after all.

Hanging onto the edge of the roof at its lowest point, Jake dropped to the ground. Again there was a sharp pain, bringing with it a surge of blood. He laid the rifle aside and drew the borrowed revolver before joining the others.

Thurston ranted at Birdie. "I'll beat you black and blue, you ungrateful little whelp!"

"Tie 'em up," Jake ordered. Walkenshaw and Grady hastened to do so.

Maybelle Walkenshaw came running up with her friend, Emily Montclaire. "Thank heaven it's over," she said.

They were herding the outlaws to their cells when Conrad and the others arrived.

"You too?" said Thurston. "I'm surrounded by traitors."

Word had gotten around and the townspeople began emerging from their homes.

"Jake, you'd better see a doctor," said Miguel.

"I'm on my way. How's Schmidt?"

"I'm sorry. He didn't make it. They left him at the undertaker's."

Jake was sorry too. Schmidt was a brave man, one who'd been willing to take a stand.

A week after the outlaws' arrest, things were settling down. Jake's wound was healing nicely and the doctor told him he could ride if he took it easy. Because of General Crook's efforts, the Apaches had withdrawn to their stronghold in the Mazatzals to the south and, for the time being, posed little threat.

To Jake's surprise, Decker had opted to stay on and start a newspaper. No doubt the decision was influenced by the charming Miss Montclaire. Walkenshaw had been appointed interim sheriff in Jake's place, and most likely he'd be elected whenever they got around casting ballots. Gebhardt and a few of his men were staying on to ensure everything went smoothly. Conrad decided to go to California. He figured he'd like the climate better. That left Birdie. Or rather Roger.

"I'm sick of being called Birdie," he'd said. "Never did like it. My name is Roger and that's what I intend to be called from now on."

No charges were brought against him since he'd killed in self-defense.

Hogue was forced to return what little of the money he had left, and was going to stand trial with the others. A judge had been sent for, along with a deputy marshal.

Jake figured he owed Birdie, or rather Roger, an awful lot and offered him a job at his ranch.

"Look, you're wanting a new start so why don't you come work for me. I'm heading south with Miguel in the morning."

Roger appeared to think that over. "I'd like that," he said at last. "Count me in. I'll be going with you."

It was right after sunup on an early October morning when Jake and his two companions left Piedmont behind them. They'd said their good-byes the night before. The gallows that Thurston and Gillaspy had ordered was left standing. It was a stark reminder that it would be used again for those who'd made it.

"I can't say I'm sad to be leaving that place," said Miguel, after a backward glance.

Jake felt the same way. He'd had more than enough of Piedmont. Now, at last, he would see Alicia and their baby daughter. At last, he was going home.